Max Cossack

Low Tech Killers

Song "One Emotion Behind" Words and Music by Joseph Vass
Copyright © 2019 Joseph Vass All Right Reserved. Included by Permission.

Other Novels by Max Cossack:
Khaybar, Minnesota
Zarah's Fire
Simple Grifts: A Comedy of Social Justice

Other books published by VWAM from Susan Vass:
Ammo Grrrll Hits The Target (Volume 1)
Ammo Grrrll Aims True (Volume 2)
Ammo Grrrll Returns Fire (Volume 3)
Ammo Grrrll Home On The Range (Volume 4)
Ammo Grrrll Is A Straight Shooter (Volume 5)

What Readers Say
about Max Cossack's consensus
5-Star Debut Novel
"Khaybar, Minnesota"

"The Most Realistic Thriller Ever."

"Frighteningly possible story, well told."

"A fast-paced pleasurable read."

"A great read, a great story and (unfortunately) extremely topical."

"You won't be able to put it down."

"Tremendous first novel."

"An entertaining tale which I enjoyed enough to read twice."

"Great read! Hard to believe this is the first book by this author. He hit all the high notes with a timely, believable plot, interesting characters and authentic dialog...Get this book, you won't be disappointed."

DEDICATION

For Carole Lager, Teacher

THOUGHTS

פְּרוּ וּרְבוּ וּמִלְאוּ אֶת־הָאָרֶץ

"(Be fruitful and multiply and fill the earth…)"

Genesis / 1:28 **בראשית**

"One has to belong to the intelligentsia to believe things like that: no ordinary man could be such a fool."

George Orwell, *Notes on Nationalism*

"Bad taste is simply saying the truth before it should be said."

Mel Brooks

"Maybe we can afford to discard the supposedly primitive superstition that insanity is caused by demonic possession. But we can't afford to discard its insight that, in action, insanity and evil are indistinguishable."

The Author

1 Lawyer Sam

"I don't google," Hack told Sam Lapidos.

Sam said, "What do you mean? You've googled hundreds of times. Or so you claimed in that fat bill you dumped on me after you investigated my Amos Owens case last summer."

"You're a lawyer," Hack said. "You ought to know that 'google' is not a generic term for searching the Internet. It is a trademark, as well as the name of a sinister corporate behemoth I hate."

Sam and Hack were sitting on opposite sides of Sam's wide ebony desk in Sam's law office, located in an old Victorian house Sam owned. about half a mile from downtown Minneapolis, on the east side of the Mississippi River.

Sam asked. "Do you use Priva-Nation for your searches? As I recall, you wrote that yourself."

"Then you should also recall that after I coded Priva-Nation and made my boss Fred Sauer almost as rich as the post-divorce Jeff Bezos, his slightly less huge but equally nasty company Gogol-Checkov canned me."

"You choose which search engine to use on personal grudges?"

"What else?"

Sam sighed. "Just out of curiosity, how do you search the Internet?"

"I use my own private search engine, USearchIT. One I coded for myself after GC fired me. With special functions and features not available in those inferior competitors."

Sam stared at Hack across his desk. "You can do that?"

"Code search engines? Somebody must be doing it, right? There are dozens out there. Now tell me, what will I be searching for?"

"Everything that might have anything to do with my case," Sam said.

"You'll have to narrow it down."

"The jackpot will be if you run across another suspect, someone I can point to at trial and create reasonable doubt for my client."

"Who's your client and what's he accused of?"

Sam leaned back in his chair and intertwined his fingers behind his head and stared at the ceiling. "His name is Richard Kadlec. In fact, he works for that former employer of yours, Gogol Checkov. Do you know him?

"No. He must have come along after GC fired me."

"Too bad," Sam said. "Well, perhaps you know someone who knows him. That would be convenient."

"I see what's going on. You're hiring me on the chance I know your client, aren't you?"

Sam ignored Hack's question. "The man they accuse him of murdering was an ostentatiously nasty right-wing windbag named Penn Lajoie, who delighted in alienating everybody in sight as he barnstormed the country sneering at the theory of man-made climate change, which my client Rick Kadlec and many others believe to the depths of their souls poses an immediate threat to all civilization and all life on earth."

"If they believe that, why do they care what he says?"

Sam said, "What really pissed them off were Lajoie's impeccable scientific credentials and his knowledge of climatology. He could spout temperature measurements and climate history at the drop of a barometer."

"They couldn't argue with him effectively?"

"He always had a better counter-argument."

"Like you."

Sam gave a modest shrug.

Hack nodded. "I see why they hated him."

Sam parted his lips slightly, displaying his shark teeth in lawyerly satisfaction at the compliment. "Exactly."

"Is this Kadlec guy guilty?"

Sam started. "Obviously not. He's my client, isn't he?"

"Did you ask him?"

Sam frowned. "Are you crazy?"

"Then how did you know he's innocent?"

2

"I didn't say he was innocent. I said he's not guilty."

'If you didn't ask him, how do you know?'"

Sam said, "Did you sleep through high school civics?"

"They dropped that requirement decades ago."

"I suspected as much," Sam said. "Look, he hasn't been proved guilty, has he?"

"They haven't even tried him yet."

"Then he's not guilty yet," Sam said. "Very much like you."

"What's that supposed to mean?"

Sam raised just one eyebrow. It was a nice trick he had. Hack was jealous. "You haven't been tried yet either."

Hack protested, "I've never even been arrested."

"So far," Sam said. "Yet few who know about you—myself, for example, or what's more serious, the feds—consider you innocent. Nevertheless, you're not guilty of anything until they prove it in court."

Hack suspected that Sam suspected that Hack might have killed somebody the previous year. Hack said, "Let's get back to your client Rick Kadlec, please. How am I supposed to help?"

"I told you, I'm hoping to come up with an alternate suspect theory," Sam said. "A Real Killer. There's bound to be at least one other suspect for killing a dickhead like Lajoie. From the defense point of view, it's what the generals call a target-rich environment."

"What's your boy Kadlec say?"

Sam shook his head. "He won't tell me anything. He doesn't care whether he's convicted."

"Seriously?"

"He sees the trial as an ideal forum to educate the public on climate and all the other upcoming catastrophes. He's willing to go down as a martyr for the Cause."

"That must be fun for you," Hack said. "What with your attorney's duty to represent him zealously and all."

Sam's mournful expression was sufficient response all by itself, but he spelled it out. "I need information. But he gives me bupkis. Nada."

Hack asked, "Have you looked at Rick's social media?"

Sam said, "Yes. One of the few things he let me in on is that he doesn't use any."

"You mean, under his own name?"

"Under any name," Sam said. "You'll see from the case file that Rick was in with a bunch of co-workers who don't tweet or follow or unfollow or any of that crap. I figure they must have hidden out somewhere else on the Internet, like the black net."

"You mean the Darknet?"

"Right. What I said."

Hack let it go.

"All kinds of terrorists and drug dealers operate there," Sam said. "It's all supposed to be hidden. Will your home brew USearchIT thingie penetrate there?"

Hack said, "As it happens, that's one of its selling points."

"Selling points? You planning to market it?"

"No. Just a figure of speech. But it's handier than TOR even."

"I won't ask what TOR is."

"Doesn't matter anyway, since I won't be using it."

"If you say so."

Hack asked, "When does the trial start?"

"Five days ago."

"This is kind of short notice, isn't it?" Hack said. "I mean, even for you."

"I tried a private investigator first," Sam said. "You know, a real one. With experience and a license and everything."

"What happened?"

"He got nowhere."

"And then you waited to hire me until after the trial started?"

4

"Well actually, I tried another licensed investigator next. She got nowhere either." Sam grabbed a handful of documents off his desk and hopped up and dashed out of the room.

Sam's abrupt exit didn't offend Hack. Sam was always walking off in the middle of conversations—sometimes conversations he himself started. You'd be at a party or in a meeting smack in the middle of telling Sam what you considered the most fascinating anecdote and you'd be just about to arrive at its hilarious punch line when Sam would think of something or remember something or simply lose interest and without a word wander away. Sam sometimes hurt the feelings of people new to him, but Hack was used to it.

It was just a matter of waiting. Either Sam would come back or he wouldn't.

Hack took advantage of the free moments to check out Sam's office. Sam had decorated the walls with photos of his wife Bea— long passed on—and Sam's daughter Lily, who happened to be Hack's ex-wife. He'd also put up a separate photo of Sam's granddaughter Sarai, who was also of course Hack's current daughter.

Bea smiled down toward Sam's swivel chair in benign toleration, as if she knew all Sam's idiosyncrasies and loved him anyway. Go figure.

Hack's daughter Sarai was smiling too. She was only ten and incredibly beautiful and still looked at the world with open relatively uncritical love, too often at the kind of jerks who in Hack's more jaded opinion didn't deserve it.

Hack's ex-wife Lily looked directly down on Hack himself. Must be one of those pictures where the eyes follow you around the room.

Although she was smiling like the others, Hack detected disapproval. During their marriage she had come to disapprove of Hack a lot. Just sitting there in Sam's office, Hack could recall dozens of good reasons.

Hack was hoping that he could keep the disapproval down to a manageable minimum with his current wife Mattie. He didn't want to screw up this marriage too.

Ten minutes. No Sam. Their meeting must be over. Hack got up and went out to the parking lot and drove the ninety minutes back home to Ojibwa City.

2 Fracas Inside "Black Powder Plot" Trial

"The personal is political AND the POLITICAL is personal."

Gaea Free, *Annals of Internal GC Struggle*

Ojibwa City *Savage*
Dateline: Minneapolis
Staff Writer Norton Shandling

A fracas erupted inside a Hennepin County District Courtroom today in the controversial trial of Richard John Kadlec. Sheriff's deputies ejected about a dozen chanting pro-Kadlec demonstrators. The deputies made no arrests.

The State has charged Mr. Kadlec with first degree murder in the car bombing of gadfly climatologist Penn Lajoie.

Professor Lajoie had grabbed national headlines with his flamboyant verbal attacks on the activists who warn of imminent climate change catastrophe. Someone planted a bomb in his Humvee this past March, just four days after a mob disrupted his speech at Ojibwa College of Minnesota.

This reporter covered the speech on behalf of the *Savage*. A small conservative group at the College sponsored the event. Some seventy people showed up, including about twenty masked protesters who claimed that, given imminent planetary catastrophe, Lajoie had no free speech right to expound what they labeled his "denialist" views.

Lajoie made a dramatic entrance. He dashed onto the lecture hall stage in an outfit straight out of 1912—checked jacket, bow tie, and straw boater. Brandishing a suitcase with the name "Prof. Harold Hill" in big light blue capital letters on the side, he launched into a song from the musical *The Music Man*:

> "We're in trouble.
> Terrible terrible trouble.

Right here in River City--
With a capital T
That rhymes with C
That stands for Climate.

Obviously befuddled, the protesters stopped waving their signs and chanting and just stared. Judging from their puzzled looks, most failed to recognize Lajoie's moldy cultural reference to the fifty-year-old movie in which a grifter scams a town's parents by convincing them the new pool hall threatens moral disaster for their children.

Lajoie had to explain his stunt. "You never saw *The Music Man*? You need to. The oldest scam in the world. Go convince a bunch of yokels they face catastrophe and only you can fix it and they better fork over their bank accounts. And that's what your global warming hysteria is—a scam."

At this, hisses sibilated from the crowd.

Then Lajoie baited them further with another outdated cultural reference, this time to the Seventies movie *Bang the Drum Slowly,* in which Major League baseball players gleefully cheat one another at a card game they call "Big League TEGWAR", standing for "The Exciting Game Without Any Rules."

Lajoie mocked the theory of anthropogenic global warming as "Big League TETWAR"—"The Exciting Theory Without Any Rules."

"To qualify as science, a theory has to be falsifiable. There's got to be some way to disprove it. If you can't test it and prove it wrong, it doesn't count as science. It's just another article of faith, a cheesy substitute for real religion."

Here Lajoie paused, as if pleased with himself. "In fact, now that I think about it, climatista science is to real science what 'cheez food' is to real cheese—you know, malleable goop squeezed out of plastic tubes."

At this point, shouts began to drown him out.

Undeterred, Lajoie lifted his arms in mock horror and waved his fingers in jazz hands. "But the theory of Global Warming, or Climate Change, or Climate Catastrophe, or whatever new moniker the liars and crackpots are using to peddle their con? There are no rules. What can't it do? If the weather's hot, that's climate change. If it's cold, that's climate change too. If there's a hurricane, or a season with no hurricanes, or famine, or drought—all routine long before toxic males charged around in SUVs and barbequed steaks—that's climate change too!"

Lajoie taunted his foes: "Don't feel too bad. I was once a sucker like you. I read that first U.N. Report, the one that says governments have only a ten-year window to solve the greenhouse effect. There was nothing we could do to stop a global three-degree temperature increase. It was just too late."

"Ten years, that's what they threatened," Lajoie shouted over the rising noise, "After ten years, it will be too freaking late."

The chants forced Lajoie to lift his voice decibels higher. "Then I noticed—I noticed, I say, I noticed—that his U.N. report was from 1989—now more than thirty years ago!"

At that, protesters began chanting, "Western Civ Has Got to Go! Settled Science tells us so!" and swarmed the stage.

In the melee, Lajoie himself was mildly injured when he sprained his right wrist punching a protester in his Guy Fawkes mask.

Four days later, on November 5, someone blew Lajoie up by putting packages of black powder under Lajoie's vintage M998 Humvee, parked in a motel lot in Minneapolis. Lajoie had just started the vehicle, planning to drive to St. Paul for an event sponsored by the American Enterprise Institute, a conservative think tank.

In the debris, police found a note claiming responsibility, signed "The Guy Fawkes Battalion."

Guy Fawkes was a conspirator who plotted to kill King James I and his Court by blowing up the British House of Lords on

November 5, 1605. Fawkes used twenty barrels of black powder, the most effective explosive of its time. Fawkes has become a role model for contemporary anarchists.

By cross-referencing different videos of the speech disruptors, conservative bloggers identified the man Lajoie punched as a local named Richard Kadlec, employed as a Relationship Analyst at St. Paul software giant Gogol-Checkov. The bloggers forwarded their information to investigators.

Prosecutors allege that when police raided Kadlec's St. Paul house, they found bomb-making equipment and radical climate-change literature. The prosecution also alleges that forensic evidence has tied the chemical signature of the bomb that killed Lajoie to the specific signature of the home-made black powder Kadlec manufactured in his basement.

As police hustled Kadlec into a squad car after his arrest, the handcuffed Kadlec yelled, "I do not recognize any authority over me of any climate-destroying capitalist court!"

Since then, Kadlec's attorney Sam Lapidos has refused all comment.

3 Intruder In The Basement

"The old world is dying, and the new one struggles to be born. Now is the time of monsters."

Antonio Gramsci

The instant Hack opened the door from his kitchen down to his basement, his eyes began to water. An acrid stench stung his nostrils and scratched its black tentacles down into his throat until he gagged.

The last time Hack had visited his own basement was a year ago the previous January, right before terrorists had slaughtered Hack's friend Amir Mohammad there and forced Hack on the run into the winter wilderness. Since then he'd balked at ever going back.

Instead Hack and his wife Mattie were spending early January in Mattie's old family house while they waited to head back to Arizona for a winter tour performing with Dudley's country music band.

This morning she had reminded him, "You've got to go back there sometime."

"Why?"

"For one thing, you own the place."

Technically that was true. His parents had left it to him. He held title free and clear. The house was his childhood home and then his adult refuge when things got tough in the outside world.

And his basement had been his refuge of refuges. He could putter at his workbench with computers and cool his insides with Chumpster beer and drown his peskiest worries in a raucous torrent of heaviest metal music. Not even a TV to disturb his solitude.

And it was also where he had left the flash drive on which he'd stored the USearchIT software he needed for the research he'd promised Sam.

Hack told Mattie, "I could sell the house."

"Not without cleaning it up first. That means getting all your crap out of there. And where would you put it? There's no room here in this bungalow."

Which was true. The one-story house Mattie had inherited from her own family was too small for both her stuff and his. It contained a tiny kitchen with a green wood table and three unsteady green-painted chairs; a living room into which she squeezed one couch, one chair and one table; a single small bedroom; and the closet that doubled as a guestroom for Sarai on weekends. The basement added just enough space for the tiny gas furnace, the washer-dryer, the laundry sink, and one funky blue couch.

Hack nodded back at Mattie and put on his coat, but he stalled in the kitchen on the way out, helpless in front of the back door.

She grabbed him by the elbows and turned him to face her. She zipped him up and patted his cheek as if he were a five-year-old resisting his first day of kindergarten. "You said you needed that flash drive. Go get it."

Hack dutifully stepped out of Mattie's house and blinked his eyes against the brilliant winter sun and the blinding whiteness of the high-piled snow and trudged the few blocks to his old home and then through the back door into his kitchen.

And when he opened the basement door, he smelled something awful.

He flicked the light switch on the wall just inside the door. He breathed through his mouth and crept downstairs to the bottom step. He waved off a few flies buzzing around his face and surveyed.

Hack turned and remounted the stairs and shut the door tight behind him and passed through his kitchen to the attached garage. He found an empty gasoline can and opened and tipped it and managed to coax a few drops of gas onto an old rag. He held the pungent rag up to his nose and took a deep whiff. Hoping he had killed his sense of smell, he stuffed the rag into a coat pocket and reversed his path back through his kitchen and down to his basement again.

This time he stepped down onto the gray concrete and wandered around. He was careful to step around the faded chalk lines where his murdered friend had lain.

Small bones littered the cement. Strings of blackened meat flecked the bones. Hack recognized a few bird claws and a single mashed robin's head, occasional scraps of white rabbit fur, and a couple of brown squirrel tails—even the single tan ankle and black cloven hoof of a deer.

He picked up an old wood yardstick from his work bench and probed a pile of scat. Mouse bones.

Something had been living here. And eating here too, and dumping its refuse.

Hack had checked all the windows and doors from the outside before he came in. The cops had sealed the entire house tight after they wrapped up their crime scene investigation the previous winter.

How could a predator big enough to bring down a deer get in? And what was it? A wolf or dog? Something smaller, like a fox? No fox could kill a deer. Though he supposed a fox could grab off a scavenged chunk of carcass and carry it home.

A bobcat or lynx? A cat might be clever enough to sneak in, but he didn't think any species of cat would foul its own lair like this.

The clatter of wood banging against metal caught Hack's attention. He turned to peer into the darkness behind the furnace. A figure sped out and sideswiped Hack and knocked him into his work bench. Hack turned and saw the creature sprinting upstairs on two legs.

The creature paused at the top of the stairs and glanced back at Hack and pushed out through the door.

The creature's pause gave Hack the chance to recognize that the creature was in fact a man and that the man wore some sort of brown fur cloak and shaggy boots. He was carrying a wooden spear with what looked like a stone point.

The pause also gave Hack a glimpse of the man's bearded face.

The glimpse was enough. Even with the spear, even under the man's beard, even under the dirt and under his skin, cracked though it was into broken red seams, even with the big broken front tooth, Hack recognized the man from Hack's years working at GC.

4 *Calvin At Large*

"We evolved to eat meat and run free."

Calvin Bagwell, *Annals of Internal GC Struggle*

Fear. Calvin runs. Up stairs. Through kitchen. Through door. Yard. Snow.

Hard breathing. Snow. Woods near. Feet thump. Houses. Trees.

Calvin stops. Cold. Warm place?

Basement warm. Now cold.

Calvin needs warm place. Knows where.

Calvin runs more.

Trees all around.

Calvin runs more.

Hard breathing. Calvin slows. Calvin walks.

More trees. Path. Shack. Little rope on door. Calvin pulls. Goes in. Warmer here. Nice. Warm. Very nice.

Food?

5 *Mattie*

"Meat eating is male. Haven't we all noticed how when we women lunch in a cozy restaurant and share the female experience, we only order healthful green salads?"

Gaea Free, *Annals of Internal GC Struggle*

"And chocolate pie chasers, no doubt."

VOR

"F*ck you, VOR!"

Gaea Free

In bed that night, Hack told Mattie about the squatter in his basement. "I'm sure I know the guy," he said. "Calvin Bagwell. I worked with him at GC."

"Another developer?" she said.

"Yes, and a good one too. He was my best friend at work for a while. Before he went all Fred Flinstone."

Hack was lying on his back, head on pillow, hands folded on his stomach, staring up at the faded ceiling wallpaper with its battling hawks and owls. The semi-transparent window curtains of their single bedroom window filtered the radiance reflected off the snow drifts outside.

Even on the bitterest winter nights, Mattie always slept naked, and Hack loved the comforting warmth of her skin as she nestled against his right arm.

She said, "What do you think he was doing in your basement?"

"I don't know. The last time I saw him was at GC. He was spouting some screwy things, but he was still wearing modern clothes. For sure I never saw him carry a spear."

"Do you think he knew that was your basement? I mean, there are a lot of basements he could have picked."

"No idea. Mine may be the only house and basement in town that's stood empty for the entire past year. Maybe that was why he picked it."

"Yeah, but why this town?" Mattie asked. "Ojibwa City's barely a dot on the map."

"Those are obvious questions," Hack agreed.

"Well to me, it seems obvious your friend knew it was your basement," Mattie said. "Which must mean something."

But Hack was thinking back to his time at GC. "And he was funny, too." Hack said. "Before he turned fanatic."

Hack said, "GC grew fast, and we had a lot of new hires wandering clueless in the corridors, so some HR genius thought up this program to help them adjust. If you were a new hire, HR picked two veterans to help you in your career development: your Mentor and your Buddy."

"I'm glad I never worked for a big company," she said. "When I started waitressing, the only training going on was me training the horny owner to keep his hands off me."

"At GC, you got a senior veteran and relatively new veteran. They called the senior veteran your Official Company 'Mentor'. The Mentor's job was to provide you guidance in company policy and politics and career development, which it turned out was pretty much the same thing as office politics."

"Sounds awful," she said.

"They assigned another person to be your Official Company 'Buddy'. They figured your Buddy could identify with your situation, being new having recently dealt with similar issues himself."

Mattie said, "That almost makes sense."

"One day Calvin and I were having a beer after work, and he claimed the HR program was incomplete. They were missing an essential additional role. He said HR should assign each new hire an Official Company 'Enemy'. It would clarify matters. You'd know right from the start who your Enemy was."

"That is kind of funny," she said.

"Would have been funnier if it didn't turn out true," Hack said. "I did acquire an Official Enemy. Her name was Tiff Madden and she made my life an Official Hell until GC threw me out."

"You've never completely gotten over that, have you?" Mattie traced her finger down his arm.

"What makes you say that?"

"You talk about it now and then, don't you?"

Hack said nothing.

She asked, "What do you think happened to Calvin?"

"I don't know. But I'd like to find out."

"Do you think you should have taken the gig working for Sam?" she asked. "We've got to head down to Phoenix for our tour in a couple of weeks."

"There's time," he said. "And the job for Sam is only for the duration of his trial, which shouldn't take too long, since Sam waited till it was already up and running before he hired me."

Mattie said, "Make you wonder, doesn't it?"

"About what?"

"About Calvin," she said. "About life, and the world, and what can happen. To anyone. Calvin had a life before he turned screwy, even before you knew him. He was some mother's baby and his parents must have loved him and they fed him and took him in for his shots and to the dentist and they paid for his education, and he got a good job, and now, if you're right that he's the same guy you saw in your basement, he's living like some kind of wild animal, and it makes you wonder—it makes me wonder, anyway. What if his parents had known that was going to happen to him?" She shivered.

"I don't know," Hack said. He was lost in his own thoughts. Troubled ones mostly, or was he was feeling a bit restless? Waiting for the tour to begin? Hard to pin down.

Memories, maybe? Triggered by seeing Calvin, from GC? Of his old life as a highly paid hotshot working for GC? And being fired?

And now out of nowhere, here's Sam representing Rick Kadlec, also from GC, on trial for murder.

Hack stared towards the ceiling a long time before he drifted into a fitful sleep.

6 *Evidence of Absence*

"Those who can make you believe absurdities can make you commit atrocities."

Voltaire, *Questions sur les Miracles a M. Claparede*

The next morning, Hack drove the ninety minutes from Ojibwa City to Minneapolis and spent the entire morning at Sam's office studying Sam's confidential case files, which included a timeline, transcribed testimony from various witnesses, and forensic analysis of the bomb and the bomb-making equipment in Kadlec's basement.

Sam's files corroborated the media reports. From the paperwork at least, Rick Kadlec looked guilty of premeditated murder.

Hack had scored a decent bankroll from his single previous investigating job for Sam. After paying off a big backlog of bills and making sure he and Mattie could eat for the near future, Hack had carved out a chunk of the excess to buy a portable but powerful laptop with the latest operating system and peripherals.

He drove back to Ojibwa City and sat at Mattie's kitchen table and used the flash drive he had retrieved from his basement to install his USearchIT software engine on his laptop.

A little effort confirmed that Sam was right: Rick Kadlec had no presence on any of the popular social media sites, at least under his own name. Since Kadlec worked for GC, the logical next step was for Hack to peek into GC's private corporate cyberspace, and since Hack was a professional who had helped design and create the original GC internal cyber architecture, it wasn't all that impossible for him to get in there and dig around.

Once in GC's network, he found a lot about Rick Kadlec, but nothing that would help Sam defend him and in fact nothing very interesting at all. GC kept the expected payroll records and performance reviews and memos, but if all Hack had to rely on were these files, Rick Kadlec was a completely unexceptional corporate drone. Hack found nothing to hint whether or why Kadlec had taken it upon himself to blow up Penn Lajoie.

Since Hack was already snooping in CG's files, he decided to satisfy his personal curiosity about Calvin Bagwell. But what he found—or rather, didn't find—caught him off guard.

Because Hack found nothing whatsoever about Calvin Bagwell. No payroll records, no reviews, no email chains, no meeting minutes, no software design documents he had written, no nothing.

A complete absence of evidence, or even existence. A nullity. Never happened. Wasn't there.

But didn't the law require GC to keep records on all its employees? Hack would double check with Sam, but he was 99% sure it did.

Which made Hack wonder. He looked for his old Company Enemy Tiff Madden. Nothing. How about himself—Nathanael Wilder? Nothing either.

GC files included hundreds of thousands of documents about employees current and former, including streams of emails circulated for internal discussions and debate as well as payroll and other employment records, going all the way back to Hack's early years, when he had helped start the company.

But it looked like GC had erased certain employees; turned them into "unpersons." They just weren't there. In fact, according to the GC files, they had never been there at all.

Did GC Management know something? Was GC's expungement of files evidence of GC's consciousness of someone's guilt, maybe even GC's own guilt?

It occurred to Hack he could identify potential Real Killers for Sam simply by nailing down which employees GC had erased. These names at least would be starting points for further investigation.

And Sam might have been right when he wondered if any of the information he'd sent Hack to hunt up might be available only on the Darknet.

But "Darknet" was just a generic term for a vast array of network services, in part a cyberspace underworld used by drug and human traffickers and terrorists, and in part a refuge for private communications. some even legitimate. It was the bulk of the Internet iceberg, underwater, and therefore unseen above the surface.

The Darknet lumped together secret bazaars for drug and weapon transactions, human trafficking sites, private friend-to-friend networks, private file transfer services, anonymous political and religious discussion groups, and sexually oriented territories whose denizens prized anonymity almost above life.

Even using Hack's own USearchIT, finding something helpful to Sam on the Darknet was a challenge. After all, to search, Hack needed something to search *for:* phrases, names, pseudonyms, groups, something. And a *place* to look would be nice—a specific private network or discussion group.

Just to make sure, Hack spent a few hours poking around a few obvious sites for references to Rick Kadlec. Nothing. Calvin? No luck. Tiff Madden or Hack himself? Nothing.

Hack had collected a bunch of reasons to hunt up Calvin in person. For starters, Calvin had kept on working for GC for some time after they fired Hack and he should know more than Hack knew about whatever went on there. Maybe he knew Rick Kadlec. Maybe he had evidence which might help Sam. Maybe he was an alternate suspect for Sam, or at least could lead to one.

And what was he doing in Hack's basement?

7 *This is ZNN: The Lajoie Interview*

"We have now sunk to a depth at which restatement of the obvious
is the first duty of intelligent men."

George Orwell

At the ZNN website, Hack found video of an interview of Penn
Lajoie conducted two days after the Ojibwa College fracas.

The interviewer was Hack's old ZNN nemesis, the reporter
Lauren Goodwell, an attractive young woman with dark swept back
hair. She was sitting behind a small desk. Hack couldn't help
noticing that female ZNN on-air personalities were universally
good-looking, while the cast of male talking heads included a lot of
bona fide toads and warthogs.

Goodwell made her trademark frowny face directly into the
camera and said, "Turmoil and chaos at a rural Minnesota College
the other night. The trigger? A speech by Penn Lajoie, the well-
known and well-compensated climate change denialist."

ZNN video told in pictures the same story the *Savage* newspaper
coverage had told in words. Protesters waved signs and chanted. A
few students yelled at them to shut up. The protesters surrounded
Lajoie and tried to drown him out. Lajoie taunted the protesters.
They rushed him. Lajoie landed an excellent right cross in the face
of a protester. The protester's black and white Guy Fawkes mask
crumpled and he went down.

Lauren Goodwell came back on camera. She said, "You may
recognize the name Ojibwa City. One year ago, this rural Minnesota
town earned international notoriety when local merchant Amir
Mohammad was murdered in what many insist was an Islamophobic
attack, and for which the chief suspect was never prosecuted."

Hack bridled. Hack had been the chief suspect. They never
prosecuted him because he'd proved he didn't kill Amir.

Goodwell continued. "I interviewed Penn Lajoie the day after the events at the College. Here is a portion of that taped interview."

Penn Lajoie stares blinking into the camera.
Goodwell: Good morning, Mr. Lajoie,
Lajoie: Good morning.
Goodwell: In your speech last night, you mocked a U.N. prediction of massive global warming?
Lajoie: Yes.
Goodwell: You do admit that major aspects of those 1989 predictions have in fact come true?
Lajoie: I don't know what you're referring to.
Goodwell: For example, in the 1989 article, the U.N. predicted events like extreme weather, wildfires, and coastal flooding that in fact have happened. So the main thrust of the 1989 article was in fact accurate, wasn't it?
Lajoie: For example?
Goodwell: In the thirty-year period before that, the Earth's surface was, on average, less than 0.2°F warmer than the twentieth-century average. In the thirty years since, the planet's surface has, on average, undergone a six-fold temperature increase.
Lajoie *(staring off into space a moment)*.

Goodwell's frowny face once again filled the screen. "As you see, Lajoie was unable to answer the kind of straightforward questions the protesters quite reasonably wanted to raise. Instead, he responded with violence. We respect freedom of speech, of course, and we would not wish to condone what Rick Kadlec is accused of doing. But we need to ask, shouldn't we draw a distinction between the kind of violence done to our planet every day, a violence that threatens the very survival of humanity, as compared to actions which a few frustrated youngsters in the heat of passion may take against this terrifying threat? Whatever Rick Kadlec may or may not have done, was it really first-degree murder, as the prosecution has charged?"

The video ended.

Goodwell's trivializing the murder of Kadlec was no surprise, but Lajoie's meekness struck Hack as odd. Lajoie wasn't a buttercup who'd let himself be pushed around.

Which raised another suspicion. For example, why was ZNN still running this interview during the trial? Did they think they had a stake in the trial outcome?

Hack didn't have to rely on ZNN's edited version of the interview. He had his trusty USearchIT software. Thirty minutes later, he put up on his screen the original unedited interview from an internal ZNN feed. ZNN's edit job was revealing, especially taking into account what ZNN removed from the original:

(Penn Lajoie stares blinking into the camera.)
Goodwell: We'll begin in a moment, Mr. Lajoie.
Lajoie: I'll be ready.
(About forty-five seconds pass.)
Goodwell: Ready now?
Lajoie: Always.
Goodwell: Good morning, Mr. Lajoie,
Lajoie: Good morning.
Goodwell: In your speech last night, you mocked a U.N. report and its predictions?
Lajoie: Yes. I did, and with good reason.
Goodwell: You do admit that major aspects of those 1989 predictions have in fact come true?
Lajoie: I don't know what you're referring to. In 1989, the U.N. predicted that within ten years ocean levels would rise three feet, that one-sixth of Bangladesh would be flooded, displacing a fourth of its 90 million people, and that a fifth of Egypt's arable land in the Nile Delta would be flooded, cutting off its food supply. In fact, none of that happened.

Goodwell: So you're saying there's no point in doing anything to prevent Climate Catastrophe?"

Lajoie: I'm not saying that. It was the U.N. that said that. In 1989, the U.N. predicted that unless action were taken by the year 2000, the situation would be irreversible. We didn't take any of the actions the U.N. insisted on, so according to them, the situation has been irreversible for at least twenty years now.

Goodwell: But wasn't the main thrust of the 1989 article correct?

Lajoie: For example?

Goodwell: For example, the 1989 article predicts events like extreme weather, wildfires, and coastal flooding that in fact have happened. Those did happen, didn't they?

Lajoie: In an amount within completely normal limits for the period. Not as the U.N. predicted, as I just explained.

Goodwell: I'm sorry, Mr. Lajoie. We have a technical glitch. Can you hang on a moment please?

Lajoie: No problem. *(staring off into space for a moment).*

Goodwell: We're back. In the 30-year period before that, the Earth's surface was, on average, less than 0.2°F warmer than the 20th-century average. In the 30 years since, the planet's surface has, on average, undergone a six-fold temperature increase.

Lajoie: That is one set of statistics from ground-based observations reported after adjustment by people who refuse to reveal any of their source data or the methods they use to make the adjustments. And yet, if we look at NASA measurements, which are much more reliable than ground-based observations, we see no warming since 2005. We also know that your selection of one particular thirty-year period is intended to obscure the undeniable fact that temperatures in the 1930's were warmer even than current temperatures.

Goodwell: That's all the time we have now, Mr. Lajoie. Thank you.

Lajoie: Thanks for having me.

8 Sarai

"Every new human being is a new crime against Mother Earth."
                    Gaea Free, *Annals of Internal GC Struggle*

Hack gave up none of his precious time with his ten-year-old daughter Sarai. If Sam's trial made him desperate, that was Sam's problem; he should have hired Hack before trial began.

Like her grandfather Sam and her mother Lily, Sarai was Jewish, and after her recent first trip to Israel, Sarai refused to ride in a car on the Jewish Sabbath, which extended from Sundown Friday to Sundown Saturday.

After sundown Saturday, Hack picked up Sarai in St. Paul and brought her back to Ojibwa City for their weekend together.

Sunday morning, Mattie made a big breakfast for all three. That afternoon, Hack took an eager Sarai and a slightly less eager Mattie out for their weekly lessons in cross-country skiing, Hack's favorite sport and only regular exercise.

One of the things Hack loved about cross country skiing was the mind-numbing solitude the winter wilderness granted him. But since first snowfall, every Sunday he sacrificed the solitude to take Mattie and Sarai along.

Hack avoided groomed and government-approved ski trails. Out past the jack pines, he knew plenty of genuine wilderness, big patches of back country he'd found on his own, the more remote the better.

By mid-afternoon he was leading Mattie and Sarai on a narrow path through the woods to one of his favorite spots. The familiar hypnotic rhythm of arms and legs in counter motion loosened and warmed him. Right leg swung with left arm, then left leg with right arm, then back again, over and over.

An occasional change in movement broke the monotony. A few times he pointed his skis outward to herringbone up a slight uphill grade or tucked them close to take it easy downhill. He loved coasting—it gave him an ease he felt he was earning as he worked his body.

He focused on his motion, the easy swing and impact of pole in snow, center of ski gripping and pushing down into snow as he kicked forward. He breathed easy and relaxed. The temperature was perfect—cool enough he didn't sweat a lot, but not so frigid as to bite.

Hack reminded himself he had a bad habit of losing self-awareness and forgetting about trail companions behind. He glanced back to make sure Sarai and Mattie were keeping up.

Sarai had her game face on, intense and focused. Strands of her dark hair poked out from under her parka and framed her sunglasses. Her small lips locked around her mouth in concentration. She was a natural in movement, lifting her legs and propelling her tiny light body smoothly behind him, already a slick little expert, keeping pace without hardship or even apparent effort.

Having started later in life, Mattie showed no visible skill, but she plugged on behind Sarai and kept up with Hack and Sarai by will power and natural strength.

Hack reached the boundary of the woods and halted. Sarai skied up alongside and stopped. Then Mattie came up behind and stopped too. Their breathing steamed the air in front them.

An expanse of unbroken snow spread out ahead, whiteness covering a meadow Hack knew from summer explorations lay underneath. A new patch of woods clustered dark on the far side, about two hundred yards away. To reach it, he would have to break trail for Sarai and Mattie. Breaking trail meant making a pair of ski tracks into which Sarai and Mattie could slot their own skis. Fine—he loved the workout.

Mattie sighed.

Hack said to her, "We can skip this if you want."

Sarai glanced up at Mattie. Mattie was just another grownup who couldn't say no to Sarai. Mattie shrugged and smiled down at Sarai and said, "Let's do it."

"All fall in," Hack shouted and stepped forward. After a few minutes of effort spent breaking trail, he reached the edge of the patch of woods on the opposite side.

These woods were denser. Clusters of dark leafless trees punctured up through white dunes of snow. A single crow lifted itself from a bare black branch into the air. It cawed a crooked course upwards and disappeared through the treetops.

Hack turned left, scouting for an easy path through.

"Hack!"

Mattie was shouting. Hack stopped and looked back. Mattie was still fifty yards behind, pointing into the woods. He shouted, "Where's Sarai?"

"You turned left and she kept going straight," Mattie shouted.

"Why?"

"She said she saw a way through. Now I've lost her."

"Where?"

Mattie pointed into the woods.

He skied back to Mattie and peered among the trees. No sign of Sarai, nor of any path high or low, just clusters of black trunks with intermittent narrow gaps among them.

He shouted, "Sarai!" but got no answer.

Hack unslung his backpack and laid it in the snow. He bent down and unsnapped his skis. He sat down and took his hiking boots out of his backpack and changed into them.

"Hurry," Mattie said.

He stood and stepped in among the pines. Mattie followed, clambering on her skis over the broken ground.

Sarai hadn't gotten far. Fifty yards in, Hack spotted a single small ski poking up out of a snowbank. She had taken a header into a snowy ditch about five feet deep. He stepped down into the depression and and brushed the snow off her shoulders and face.

She grinned up at him. "Hi, Dad."

"Didn't I teach you to stay right side up?"

"Just resting."

"Did you hurt yourself?"

"No."

"You sure?"

"I'd know."

He brushed more chunks of loose snow off her legs and her body until he exposed her torso and grabbed her by her small shoulders. He lifted her light body upright and with ease held her out at arm's length. Her eyes were level to his. He made a show of inspecting her up and down.

"Not hurt, Dad. Snow is soft."

He asked, "I'm glad I taught you how to fall."

"Falling's fun too."

"A ten-year-old's idea of fun," he said.

"I am ten."

"You have a way of making me forget."

"You can put me down now," she said.

"Promise to stay right side up?"

"For now."

Hack ignored his daughter's laughing complaints and hugged her to his chest and carried her over the uneven ground out of the woods and set her skis-first on the snow. He sat down and swapped his hiking boots for his own ski boots and skis.

One glance at Mattie's constricted face told him what to say next. "I think that's enough for today. We'll head back."

Sarai said, "Do we have to?"

Hack gave Sarai a shrug in Mattie's direction.

Mattie's face was white and bloodless, her eyes wide, her lips trembling.

Sarai grabbed Mattie's hand. "Nothing happened, Mattie. I'm fine. It was fun."

Mattie said nothing, just bent down and hugged her.

Sarai looked under Mattie's shoulder at Hack with questioning eyes.

Hack lifted the tip of one mitten to his lips to signify "Quiet" and placed the other on Mattie's shoulder. He said, "All is fine. Everybody's okay."

Mattie shrugged Hack's hand off her shoulder. She said, "Let's go," and started home. Hack waved Sarai to follow Mattie and brought up the rear all the way back.

Nobody spoke. By the time they reached Mattie's bungalow, it was late afternoon, almost sunset on this short January day. The sun glowed low and red in the sky.

Mattie got there first. Sarai followed Mattie through the back door into the kitchen and Hack followed Sarai. By that time, Mattie had already stripped off her outdoor gear. Barefoot in jeans and tee shirt, Mattie walked stiff legged into the living room. Hack heard their bedroom door snick shut from the other side of the living room. Sarai and Hack took off their own gear and collected Mattie's off the kitchen floor and stowed all the gear properly in the little standalone garage behind the house.

Back in the kitchen, Hack boiled some water and made two cups of cocoa. He and Sarai sat silent at the table while they waited for the cocoa to cool. Sarai took a cautious sip and asked, "Dad, what's wrong with Mattie?"

"She's upset, that's all."

"I see that. But why? Nothing happened to me at all."

Hack said, "Maybe it's because she lost her own daughter."

"You never told me that."

"There was never a good time. I wasn't sure you were ready."

Sarai said, "When did you think I would be?"

"Never, I guess. I know I'm not."

Sarai asked, "What happened?"

"I don't know the details. She had a two-year-old daughter named Teddi who drowned. That's all I know."

"You don't know how it happened?"

Hack shook his head.

Sarai asked, "Did she tell you about it?"

"No, other people did."

"You never asked Mattie herself?"

"No. I've opened doors, but she's never walked through. I just let it alone. She'll talk if and when she wants to."

Sarai's eyes misted. She sat silent while they both sipped their cocoa.

Sarai said, "Everybody's always telling me it helps to talk about bad things that happened. To get over them. Do you think it does?"

"No idea," Hack said. "Maybe. But what if you dwell on something and make it the whole story of your life? That could harm you too."

"I suppose," she said.

"But the truth is I don't really know. Could be one of those things that experts say, but I don't have a lot of confidence in people who call themselves experts. So I don't know."

His daughter eyed him. "You say that a lot, don't you? That you don't know?"

"Do I? I didn't know that."

They went back to their silence.

After a few minutes, Sarai pushed back her chair and stood. "Maybe I should go talk with Mattie."

"About Teddi?"

"Of course not. About me. That I'm fine. It was fun. She doesn't have to worry or be sad about me. Do you think that might help her?"

"I don't know," he said.

Sarai went into the living room. From the other side of the living room came the sound of a gentle knock, a few murmured words and then a door opening and closing.

Hack got a can of Chumpster beer from the fridge and snapped the top open. He made himself a turkey and swiss sandwich and set it on a small white plate. He carried his snack downstairs to the basement and plopped down on Mattie's ancient blue couch and sipped from his beer bottle and ate his sandwich and stared at her laundry sink and her washer dryer and her little gas furnace.

Poor Mattie.

Poor Calvin.

Poor everyone.

Except you.

You're the lucky one. You're the luckiest man alive—maybe ever. You've got a fierce and loving wife, a wise and beautiful daughter, money coming in, warm dry shelter, and plenty to eat and drink. One of the luckiest ever.

With no savings worth counting, you're still flourishing in wealth, at the top one percent of all the humans who ever lived in all the eons of human history and prehistory. How many of them could grab a sandwich and an ice cold beer and hunker down with both in a warm dry place, anytime they felt like it?

But of course, there was always the nagging worry. What might happen to Sarai? Should you keep on letting her take headers in the woods on her own? Or guard her the way every cell of your being screams at you to guard her?

You've seen the sheltered kids, the darlings whose mommies and daddies flutter around them, lecturing and hectoring, harassing teachers for the best grades and best schools.

Hack had seen a mother strap a helmet onto her dear little prince before letting him climb onto a pogo stick. How could that kid ever learn how to fall right? To land without smacking his head on the pavement? Or to jump up and start bouncing on his pogo stick all over again? How could a kid never hit in the face with a dodge ball or who never fell out of a tree or took a dive into a snow drift learn what she'd need later to survive?

Reminded him of what Gus Dropo had said: "You want Sarai to be safe? Help her grow up strong." That was certainly Gus's way with his own son LG.

Which put him in mind of some of the new hires he'd run into at GC, who couldn't deal with criticism or adversity because they'd never experienced anything negative.

Which in turn made him flash on memories of Gus and himself as kids and what they'd done and seen. At first, he smiled to himself, but, on reflection, he shuddered.

Hack didn't like words like "snowflake" hurled at people who complained of pain, no matter how invisible that pain might be to him or any other outsider. He reminded himself he wasn't qualified to judge the trauma of others.

But.

Take Tiff Madden, for example. His former GC coworker. His Enemy. The Chief Complainer. She knew a lot about social and cultural theories and nothing whatsoever about software. Maybe thought it came from the same place she imagined iPhones came from. Or electricity. Or food, for that matter.

Couldn't code her way out of a wet paper bag, though as he recalled, no one at GC had ever asked her to code even a single line. Hack knew this because he'd been in a big design meeting with her and the discussion had forced him to explain what if-then-else logic was, at which she snapped at him that he was "mansplaining."

Then there was the incident which Hack had thought at the time to be trivial. And wasn't.

Tiff's cubicle shared an aisle with his, three cubicles down and across. He was working through lunch. He had just peeled a banana and stuck its tip into his mouth.

For reasons Hack couldn't figure at the time, Tiff sometimes wore wooden shoes. On her way somewhere, Tiff clonked by. She was braless, in a microscopic tee shirt dyed a pink which matched her hair color *du jour*. Naturally he heard her, and just as naturally he glanced up. Their eyes met for an instant, then he went back to work.

That was the whole thing.

Two days later, HR called him in for a meeting with three affable HR snots, one of whom informed him across a very large table in a very somber tone that some unnamed person had registered an anonymous complaint against him, for "ogling."

Of course, Hack knew who it was.

The only one of the three amiable robots to speak was Blondie in the center. She spoke in a mild pleasant voice as she cross-examined him over the "ogle"—he foolishly admitted the event but told her it was accidental—and she seemed noncommittal at his response, though she did wonder why it was also reported that the eye contact had lasted longer than the permitted five seconds.

Blondie went on to mention that she and many unnamed others had noticed that Hack never chimed in on the email chains or in the meetings at which everyone universally touted GC's commitment to social justice and diversity and inclusion. She certainly hoped that Hack shared that commitment. In a supportive and encouraging way Blondie suggested he find ways to draw attention to his support for it. Doing this could only help his relations with other GCers.

She asked him some other questions too, about Gogol Chekhov's "mission" and how he saw himself fitting in.

Hack thought it was GC's mission was to make money from computer software, and his job was to code it. He said so.

The three HR reps shared looks with one another and she ended the meeting. Hack left with a feeling of unease, as if he had failed the exam without being told what the test question was. Though of course he knew.

He hadn't paid much attention to Tiff before—she hadn't been on many of the same projects—but now he began to see Tiff's name everywhere. She was a prominent voice in the email chains, meetings and position papers touting GC's role as a "force for social and cultural transformation." Nobody ever specified transformation to what.

About a week after the meeting with HR, Hack found an anonymous yellow post-it-note on his desk, accusing him of

"Islamophobia." He scrambled his brains to imagine what he could have said, but the closest he could come was a casual conversation in which he had suggested that some Ojibwa College beauty queen who refused to try on a Muslim head scarf had done nothing wrong, it being "her head and her hair." Somehow that translated into "disparaging" a religion—a religion about which he had no feelings whatsoever, all religions being equally irrelevant in his indifferent eyes.

What followed was an escalating campaign of suspicion, whispers, shunning, and ultimately terror. It was like the old English poem Hack had read in school, written by a courtier King Henry The Whatever had stripped of his title: "They flee from me that sometime did me seek."

Nothing had changed in the 500 years since Thomas Wyatt wrote that line. Almost instantaneously Hack sped from minor corporate celebrity to hated pariah without passing through nonentity. Now no one, not even Calvin, dropped by Hack's cubicle for a casual conversation or an invitation to lunch.

And HR was watching. Very soon Hack's secretly documented "lack of commitment to diversity and inclusion and social justice" supplied the lubricant to grease his inevitable expulsion down the skids and out the door.

Looking back, Hack was glad he was out of GC, although he would have preferred that the getting out be voluntary. He had learned something important—maybe the most important thing he'd learned so far: he had things to do more meaningful than squinting at a screen and clacking on keys to make rich people even richer.

Hack took the final swig of his beer and stood. He climbed up the stairs to the kitchen and threw the can in the garbage sack in the can under the sink and headed through the living room towards the bedroom. He opened the door and in the dim snowlight through the window he saw Mattie asleep on her side, still in her jeans and tee shirt, and Sarai asleep next to her, Sarai's arm, long and small, flung protectively over Mattie's back.

Hack nudged the door shut as quietly as he could and went back down to the basement couch to spend the night.

9 Gus and Shakey Dropo

"I think I could turn and live with animals…
They do not sweat and whine about their condition,
They do not lie awake in the dark and weep for their sins,
They do not make me sick discussing their duty to God."

Walt Whitman, Song of Myself

Hack's best friend Gus Dropo was the man to help find Calvin. Monday morning Hack dropped Sarai off at her school in St. Paul and drove back towards Ojibwa City. Just short of town he turned off County 15 for Gus's family acreage on the edge of the jackpines and drove the long gravel path to Gus's house and parked in his dirt back yard.

Hack didn't bother to knock at Gus's back door. He found Gus sitting at his kitchen table nursing a late morning Chumpster. Hack grabbed his own cold Chumpster bottle out of the fridge and sat down with Gus and explained he'd like Gus's help finding his former co-worker Calvin.

"You got those skis of yours," Gus said. "What do you need me for?"

"Superior woodcraft?"

"You know these woods almost as well as me," Gus said.

"Company?"

A white husky with bright blue eyes strolled into the kitchen. He stood about knee high and looked to weigh about fifty pounds. Hack lowered his open left hand and the big puppy came over and sniffed at it and licked the back of it a couple of times.

Hack asked, "Who's this?"

"Shakey," Gus said. "Our new Dropo."

"Shakey? Because of that trembling thing he's got going on?"

"The vet calls it an idiopathic tremor."

"What does that mean?"

"Shakey shakes his head and nobody knows what causes it and it won't go away. But a little of this seems to help." Gus leaned down and poured some of his Chumpster into a bowl on the floor.

Shakey went straight for the beer and lapped it up with noisy doggy enthusiasm.

"He'll fit right in," Hack said.

Gus said, "Another reject, but unlike the rest of us Dropos, all the sex that led up to him was thought out ahead of time. So he's purebred. But his finicky breeder decided his tremor made him defective and dumped him at the animal shelter."

Shakey finished his beer and looked up with bright blue eyes and whined something.

Gus answered Hack's questioning look: "Huskies don't bark. They speak in other voices."

"How'd you wind up with him?"

"LG wanted a dog and I said 'Okay, but you pay for it' and LG picked him up for twenty bucks and a couple of hundred for the shots." Gus shook his head. "Of course, now it's me paying the vet to treat the tremor."

"Sounds about right. Where is LG, by the way?"

"Two-week math camp," Gus said. "He says it'll help him at the U next year."

"Plus he gets some time away from you."

"It's a healthy break for both of us." Then, "So where will we look for this caveman friend of yours?"

"He's got to have some hideaway from the cold somewhere."

"How about our shack?" Gus asked. "That's shelter."

"How would Calvin know about it?" Hack asked.

Gus said, "The same way we find out about things out there. He'd look."

"I suppose it's a place to start."

The two finished their beers and bundled up and hiked forty minutes through the woods to their shack. Shakey ran along with them, sometimes rushing ahead and sometimes hanging behind, continually checking out the fascinating woodsy smells.

Back in high school, Gus and Hack had built their seven-by-ten-foot shack together, using a few sheets of plywood and tar paper and various scraps salvaged from an even older shack. It perched near the border of a plot of land the Dropo family had owned for generations. It was rickety and unpainted and had no electricity. It was perfect.

Hack and Gus made a teenage pact never to bring anyone else there, not even girls. It was a private place for two boys to hang out while they snuck their first beers and smokes.

Aside from the few months he spent on a football scholarship at the U—a scholarship he abandoned—Gus had never lived away from home. After GC fired Hack and Hack moved back to Ojibwa City, the shack once again became their private hideaway, this time for two at least slightly more grown-up men. Their only upgrade was a small propane stove.

As Gus and Hack approached the shack, they spotted a cluster of gouges in the snow all around it, obviously footprints, wide edges blurred. Shakey dashed from print to print, sniffing each one.

The shack's vertical plywood door hung down from two rusty hinges only four feet off the ground. The handle was a short piece of rope. Gus took off one mitten and drew a forty caliber Glock pistol from under his coat and, extending his trigger finger along the slide, with the barrel pointed down, he looked his question at Hack.

Hack nodded assent. You never could tell.

With his mittened hand Gus pulled on the rope to lift the door and ducked inside, his huge frame bent nearly double. From inside, he called, "Clear."

Hack ducked in and let the little door fall close behind him. Stuck outside, Shakey began whining with dogged persistence until Hack lifted the door again. Shakey dashed inside and sprinted around, inspecting the quarters.

The shack wasn't as messed up as Hack's basement, but on the ground lay another small chunk of leg bone from what might have been the same deer, along with scattered smaller bones and Calvin's trademark fur patches. Shakey sniffed once at the deer bone, ignored the other stuff, and curled up in one corner to watch the men.

Gus fired up the propane stove while Hack policed the space. He gathered the garbage and stuffed it into one of the green ten-gallon lawn disposal bags the men kept there. He tied the bag at the top and set it outside by the door to let winter lock its contents solid in the sub-freezing air. He let the little door fall closed.

Hack said, "We can take that crap back to your house and get rid of it from there."

"Okay," Gus said.

They unfolded their two old wooden slat chairs and sat. In a few minutes, the tiny space heated up enough for them to take off their coats and mittens. They leaned back and stretched their legs to warm their feet near the stove.

"It's nice Calvin found shelter here," Hack said. "I suppose I don't even mind."

"It would have been even nicer if your pal had cleaned up after himself," Gus said.

"He's not my pal. At least not anymore," Hack said. "He's just someone I have a lot of questions for."

"After we warm up in here, we'll follow his trail easy in the snow," Gus said. "We'll find him and then you can ask him all your questions."

"Good," Hack said. "Now I've got a question for you." The thought had been nagging at him. "You know Mattie about as well as me."

"Not really."

"I thought you two got close when LG was little. After her daughter Teddi died."

"Close, yeah, but not close like you. She was never my wife or lover or anything. We were just friends, as they say. She helped me out a lot with LG after Teddi drowned."

"I didn't know that," Hack said. "I kind of assumed—"

"Another question you never bothered to ask."

Wrong again, Hack reflected, with some irritation at himself. Always one step behind with Mattie. And Gus too. "Well, I think she had some kind of a flashback episode yesterday," Hack said. He told Gus about Sarai's skiing mishap and Mattie's agitation.

"Rough," Gus said.

"Yes."

Gus began, "Well, I'm not unduly sensitive—"

"—You're not even duly sensitive," Hack interrupted.

"Nice little zinger, there, Partner," Gus said. "Anyway, I see how that could happen. You remember, she used to erupt a lot more before you two hooked up. Losing her kid is about the worst thing there is, and she was really broken to pieces."

"I can't imagine," Hack said, thinking of Sarai.

"Don't," Gus said, and Hack guessed he was thinking of LG. "Maybe the scare with Sarai set off a memory. Like PTSD."

"I figured that much."

"But just stay with her and she'll work it out."

"Of course I'll stay with her," Hack said. "She's my wife."

"I don't mean just that," Gus said, "I mean stay with her emotionally. Consider her feelings. Pay attention. Listen to her."

Hack said, "So now, between the two of us, you're the voice of empathy for women?"

"Shows how far you've fallen," Gus said, and stood up.

Gus turned off the stove and they put on their outdoor gear again and left the shack to follow Calvin's trail deeper into the woods. Shakey followed.

The trek wasn't far, but in some places deep snow drifts slowed them. About two hours later, they tracked Calvin's prints to a small bluff overlooking a frozen creek about six feet across. A dark hole about eight feet wide opened in the bank on the other side.

Somewhere along the way Shakey had disappeared.

"I didn't know we had caves around here," Hack said.

"It's not a cave," Gus said. "I should have thought of this place before. My grandfather showed it to me. It's a mine shaft."

"What were they mining?"

"Not they. He. A French trapper named Marceau Mortimer."

"When was this?

"A couple of centuries ago. This Marceau Mortimer was hunting for the Northwest Passage, you know, the overland trail explorers never found from the Atlantic to the Pacific. Claimed he was a Marquis, a nobleman, chased out of France in one of their revolutions. Nobody believed that. The Ojibwa had a name for him. Called him"—Gus uttered a phrase Hack didn't catch.

"What was that?"

"His name in Ojibwa."

"What does it mean?"

"Lost Frog."

"Frog as in Frenchman?"

"Of course not. Sometimes I wonder what goes on in your head. No ethnic slur intended. By the Ojibwa anyway. The frog was Marceau Mortimer's spirit animal. But the trappers around here just called him Morty Mark."

"You don't say."

"I do say," Gus said. "Anyway, after Morty Mark's winery failed—he kept trying to grow one varietal after another, Cabernet Sauvignon, Pinot Noir and so on—wine grapes here in the northland jackpines, if you can believe—no business sense really, just one foolhardy scheme after another. Then, for no reason anybody else could see, this Morty Mark decided there must be gold hereabouts and dug that little mine shaft we're looking at."

"Gold in Minnesota?"

Gus shook his head. "Everybody told him he was crazy. Like with the winery."

"Did he find any gold?"

"Some said yes, some said no, some just shook their heads."

Hack shook his own head. "What happened to him?"

"My grandfather told me he moved to St. Paul and started a brewery. Had some mysterious source of wealth to invest. Never told anyone where he got it. Died rich. Turns out Minnesota is beer country, not wine country."

"So he did find gold after all?"

Gus said, "If he did, the vein played out. I dug all around in there when I was a kid and I didn't find anything but a few rabbit bones and a whole lot of bat droppings."

"That's quite a tale," Hack said. "Almost impossible to believe."

"Almost," Gus agreed. "Anyway, your buddy Calvin is not the first wacko to take up residence in that hole in the ground."

"Should we go say 'Hi, Wacko'?" Hack asked. He took a step down the little slope to the creek.

Gus laid one hand on his arm. "This Calvin's got a spear, you said?"

"Good point."

"I won't make the obvious joke," Gus said. "But we can't just stumble into a man's private cave. I've heard cavemen can be unduly sensitive. We'll approach with caution."

Keeping his feet, Gus slid his bulk down the icy slope and Hack followed one careful step at a time. They found a flat spot about fifteen yards to the right of the shaft and stamped with care across the frozen creek. They moved as quietly as they could along the lower ground of the bank until they were only a few yards from the dark shaft opening.

"Now what?" Hack said.

Gus took off a mitten and stuffed it into an outside coat pocket and took his Glock from under his coat again.

Hack said, "This time we're pretty sure it's Calvin in there. We won't need that."

"Good to know," Gus said. He moved the pistol down behind his butt. But he didn't put it away.

Wind had swept most of the snow off the narrow bank. Hack took careful steps along the hard-frozen ground towards the shaft opening. When he got to about ten feet away he could see the front area of the shaft. Dark ashes lay on top of a small pile of blackened rocks.

Gus came up behind Hack.

Hack said in a low voice, "He built himself a fire, but it's out."

"A fire in a cave in winter is risky," Gus said in a matching low voice. "If there's water in the rocks above and the heat of your fire melts the ice, the rocks can break. Then the pieces fall on your head and kill you."

"But you said this is a mine shaft, not a cave."

"A mine shaft in rocky frozen ground," Gus said.

"I don't see any fallen rocks."

"Calvin doesn't know what he's doing, is my point," Gus said. "Any real caveman would know what I just said. Living outdoors requires knowledge too, probably more than hunching in a cubicle in some office tower noodling letters and numbers."

"Don't forget special characters," Hack said. "Anyway, I know that."

"And he doesn't," Gus said.

Hack stepped forward and Gus followed. Hack stopped just short of the opening, He called, "Calvin!"

No answer.

"Calvin!" then, "It's Nathanael Wilder. Remember me?"

A hoarse voice came out of the dark shaft. "Hack Wilder?'

"Yes. Do you remember me?"

"Sure."

"I'd like to talk with you. You got some time?"

"Nothing but."

Gus poked Hack in the back.

Hack said, "I have a friend with me. May we both come in?"

Out of nowhere, Shakey appeared. He sprinted past Gus and Hack into the cave.

Calvin shouted, "Didn't say wolf!"

"He's not a wolf; just a dog. A husky. He's friendly. His name is Shakey. I didn't realize he'd come along with us. May we come in?"

Calvin coughed. "Sure. Lonely. Long time. No guests."

Hack stepped forward to the front of the opening. Gus came right behind. One hand was mittened and the other bare, but his gun was out of sight.

The stink was Hack's basement all over again, putrid, musty, and moldy.

The outdoor light from behind Hack and Gus showed Calvin sitting cross-legged just in front of the back wall, about fifteen feet in. Scrawny reddened ankles jutted out beneath the dark fur cloak draping down over most of him. His bare left hand gripped his wooden spear, propped up against the wall. Bright blue eyes peered out from his bearded face.

Shakey squatted on his haunches a yard to Calvin's left, staring at the man.

"Nice wolf," Calvin said to Shakey.

Shakey stepped forward and licked Calvin's hand.

"This is my friend Gus," Hack said.

"Hello, Gus," Calvin said. He coughed again.

"Hello, Calvin," Gus said.

"And Shakey," Hack said.

"Hello, Shakey," Calvin said. He reached over and rubbed Shakey's head. Shakey nuzzled Calvin's hand in acceptance of the greeting.

"I've been worried about you," Hack said. "Since I saw you in my basement."

"Sorry," Calvin said. Hack realized there was something different about Calvin's voice. It was more guttural, maybe, as if he'd been taking diction lessons from caveman movies.

"No need to be sorry," Hack said.

Calvin said, "Against rules."

"Rules?"

"No modern housing. Live in the wild, paleo."

"I see," Hack said, although he didn't. But he began to remember some of the conversations back at GC that had begun to disconnect Calvin and himself.

Calvin said, "Caught outdoors. Far from home. Emergency, Temporary solution." A bout of coughing seized him. The coughing turned to a paroxysm which convulsed him.

"You okay?" Hack asked.

"Fine," Calvin rasped out.

"Anytime you need a place to stay, go ahead and use my basement, no problem," Hack said.

"Thanks," Calvin said.

Hack said. "Or our shack, if it's closer."

Gus poked a thick stiff finger into Hack's side, blunt and hard as a pistol barrel. Hack hoped it wasn't one.

"Thanks," Calvin said again. His coughing stopped.

Shakey began licking Calvin's beard. Calvin made no move to stop him or even to avoid the slurping. He just stared at Hack and Gus.

Gus spoke up. "Paleo?"

Calvin fixed Gus with an appraising stare. "Kindred?"

"To a point," Gus said.

Calvin asked, "Live like a man?"

"To a point," Gus said.

"Eschew wreckage of civilization. Follow biology. Our evolutionary nature."

Hack said, "Our nature?"

Calvin mustered a complete sentence. "We evolved to eat and run wild. Hunt. Eat what we hunt."

"I see," Hack said. More of Calvin's speeches in his GC cubicle came back.

"No vegetables," Calvin said. "Not healthy."

Hack said. "Well, I'm glad to see you're okay."

"Am," Calvin said. He pointed to a pile of meat scraps on the ground in front of him. "Share."

"I had a really big breakfast right before I came," Hack said.

Gus said, "Me, too."

Shakey grabbed a few of the multi-colored chunks off the ground and gobbled.

Hack said, "But I was wondering about Rick Kadlec."

Calvin gave a solemn nod. "Sad."

"Sad?"

"Sad. Very sad. What Tiff did."

"What Tiff did?"

Calvin nodded.

"Tiff did something to Rick?"

Calvin just stared at Hack.

Hack said, "Which was?"

Calvin said, "Don't know?"

Hack shook his head.

"I'm tired," Calvin said.

To Hack, Calvin looked it. And worse. Hack asked, "Can we help you in some way? Do something for you? Take you somewhere?"

"Better off here," Calvin hacked out. Bubbles of phlegm appeared at his lips. Shakey licked them off.

Hack said, "Can we maybe bring you something?"

"No," Calvin said. "No processed food. Corrupt societal infrastructure. Nothing from you at all. Nothing personal."

"Calvin," Hack said. "You can help me out. Rick is in big trouble. They're prosecuting him for murder. They say he killed a man."

Calvin showed some interest. "Who?"

"A climate scientist named Penn Lajoie."

"Oh, yeah." Calvin shrugged. "How?"

Interesting he would ask how. Hack said, "Blew him up with black powder."

Gus put in, "The murderer didn't use any modern plastic explosive or anything like that. Do you know why that was?"

"Principles," Calvin said.

"Whose principles?" Gus asked.

"Guy Fawkes Battalion," Calvin said.

Hack circled back. "Tell me, please, what did Tiff do to Rick?"

But Calvin had lost interest. He shrugged.

"It might help a Rick a lot," Hack said.

Calvin looked sad. "No help for Rick."

"Why not?" Hack asked. "Why is there no help for Rick?"

"Ask Tiff," Calvin said. He appeared to consider a moment, then his lips opened in a kind of snarky expression, displaying his broken front tooth. "Or ask Gaea Free."

"Gaea Free?"

"Tired," Calvin said. "Time sleep."

"Who's Gaea Free?" Hack asked.

But Calvin leaned against the back wall and laid his spear across his crossed legs and closed his eyes.

Shakey lay down and nestled his head on Calvin's thighs and closed his eyes too.

They both began snoring.

Gus poked Hack. "I think he's out for now."

Hack said, "Calvin?"

"We're not to get any more out of him," Gus said.

Hack said again, "Calvin?"

Gus tugged at Hack's arm and said, "This hole is hazardous to our health." Gus turned and walked out through the shaft opening and turned left. Hack turned and started to follow.

"Hack!" Calvin said.

Hack turned back. Calvin's eyes were open. He said, "Write?"

Hack took of his right mitten and reached under his coat and took out his phone.

Calvin gave him a string of letters, number, and special characters, then he said, "Dot Onion."

Hack had been keying as Calvin spoke. "Got it. Do I need a password?"

Calvin gave him a shorter string of letters, numbers and special characters. Calvin closed his eyes and in an instant was snoring even louder than before. Shakey stirred a bit and eyed Calvin, then closed his eyes again.

Hack left the shaft and joined Gus, who was waiting a few yards away by the creek.

"What was that about an onion?" Gus asked.

"A location on the Dark Web," Hack said. "Darknet website names are randomly generated strings of characters that end with the word 'onion'."

"Why?"

"No idea."

Gus asked, "But you got something useful out of him, right?"

"I'll know for sure when I get home," Hack said.

They crossed the creek and hiked up the slope.

At the top, Gus stopped and said, "Proves one thing."

"What's that?"

"They say that to a dog there's no such thing as a bad smell. Shakey proves it."

"You going to just leave Shakey behind with Calvin?"

Gus said, "Shakey's choice."

"Is that why he doesn't even have a collar? You're letting him make his own decisions?"

"He knows where he lives. And where his beer is."

As they trudged through the snow back to the Shack, Hack said, "Hearing Calvin just now, I started remembering some of the discussion he and I used to have. He was big into this Paleo thing. That we should eat like our Paleolithic ancestors ate for millions of years, back in the old stone age, lots of red meat, no farm products. No processed food."

"And now he's taken it the next logical step. Trying to live that way too," Gus said.

"He was always a very logical guy. Very consistent in his reasoning. That's one reason he was a good programmer."

"He's batshit crazy."

"That's a bit strong. Maybe he just got carried away with a crazy idea. He's like that. That doesn't make him actually insane."

"No, I mean batshit for real. Didn't you hear him coughing? I told you that mineshaft is full of bat guano. There's a fungus grows on bat droppings. You breathe in the spores and it wrecks your lungs."

"Lung disease doesn't automatically make a man crazy."

"It does if his brain doesn't get enough oxygen. And the fungus can infect the brain too."

Hack pondered that a moment. Then he said, "Must be something we can do for him."

"What?" Gus said.

"Don't know. Can't live like that," Hack said. "Paleo."

"Actually, he can." Gus said. "People lived exactly like that for at least a million years. Hunting."

"Don't forget gathering," Hack said.

From behind, Shakey dashed by them. About thirty yards past he stopped and looked back at the two men as if waiting for them to catch up.

Gus said, "A million years ago there were only a few thousand people on the whole planet at any particular time. Seven billion humans can't all live just from hunting. We need farms."

"Know."

"Calvin is not your problem," Gus said. "You should butt out."

"Know."

"This country's still mostly free, at least out here in these woods. Let him live and die how he wants. By the way, do you know who this Gaea Free is?"

"No."

"You're getting pretty short-winded yourself, Partner," Gus said.

"Huh?" Hack said. "You're right. He's got me doing it too."

"You've always talked too much anyway," Gus said. "I like your new approach. Stick with it as long as you can."

"Will."

The truth was that Hack's wandering thoughts had distracted him from Gus. Hack knew that Calvin's enthusiasm for the "paleo" life—at least as a theory—had developed long before Calvin took up residence in a hole in the ground.

Hack remembered Calvin's progressively more intense fervor as he dropped by Hack's GC cubicle nearly every day to declaim each new development in his research and his theories: "Don't you get it? We're living false lives. We've lost touch with our true nature. We evolved on the African Savannah, running down antelope, fighting it out with lions and leopards. We did that for a million years."

"Maybe two million," Hack said.

"Right, two million," Calvin said. "And how long have we farmed? Maybe five thousand years."

"More like ten thousand," Hack said, "But I get your point."

Calvin's eyes glowed. "Right. A tiny percentage of all the centuries human beings have been around. And it's not just farm food that's unhealthy. What about the shoes?"

"Shoes?"

"Evolution designed us to go barefoot, Hack. Think about it!"

And so on.

And scary, even at the time. And not just because of the personal danger to Calvin if he started trying to live according to his theories—a danger Hack had just now seen come to life in old Morty Mark's mine shaft.

Hack had experienced a mild example at GC when Tiff Madden had managed to gin up the cyber mob against himself.

After the experience, Hack dug into a lot of history books. It turned out his own nasty experience was a mere blip, as were all the relatively pipsqueak current phenomena like "twitter mobs" and "cancel culture." These were small stuff—lower-case history compared to the big capital "H" History books Hack had been reading.

The big History of humanity was a History of cults, frameups, show trials, lynch mobs, pogroms, Japanese POW camps, mass rapes, the Chinese Cultural Revolution, the Nazi Holocaust, the Killing Fields of Kampuchea, the Rwandan genocide, the Muslim conquest of the Mideast, mutual mutilation and massacre by American settlers and Indians, communist gulags, fascist torture, socialist death squads, internment of Japanese Americans, ten thousand years of human slavery, and the almost forgotten fourteenth century Muslim conquest of India, which killed something like eighty million people.

Reading all this History had spurred Hack even more in his natural inclination towards hermitry. People were just plain scary, especially in groups.

In trying to explain this History, the historians seemed to fall into two camps. Either they blamed social forces like capitalism and feudalism or they blamed individual human failings like greed and lust and envy, the same tired sins prophets had inveighed against throughout time. No wonder the prophets had decided to stop bothering to show up.

Maybe. But Hack wondered about the role of the human mind, the mind's capacity to enchant itself with a Big Idea, allowing one to think oneself into doing things crazy or stupid or evil or all three at once.

Had Calvin thought himself into huddling almost naked in a stinking mine shaft?

Had something like that happened to Sam's client Rick Kadlec? Had Kadlec thought himself into planting a bomb?

More to the immediate point: what about Hack himself? Was he thinking too much? Maybe it was time he put aside the paralysis of investigating and researching and do something useful—one single good thing for one single person.

It didn't look like Calvin would last out the month of January. Despite Gus's wise advice to butt out, Hack was trying to think up a way to butt in.

10 Sam at Trial: The Expert Witness

"Trial by jury is a privilege of the highest and most beneficial
nature...our most important guardian both of public and private
liberty. The liberties of England cannot but subsist so long as this
palladium remains sacred and inviolate."

William Blackstone

"Trial by jury is the palladium of our liberties. I do not know what a
palladium is, but I am sure it is a good thing."

Mark Twain

The next morning, Hack took a few hours off his investigation to
drive down to Minneapolis and check on Sam's trial. Hack parked in
an underground garage and took the elevator up to the level of the
Minneapolis Skyway, a concourse which allowed people to travel
and shop the entire downtown indoors. He walked through the
Skyway past the US Bank Plaza Building to the Hennepin County
Government Center. He passed through security to the Court Tower
and took an elevator up.

A thin woman lawyer and her male client shared Hack's
elevator. Hack pegged the woman as a lawyer by her shabby gray
suit and the dour resigned look on her face. He ID'd the runt with
her as her client from his unkempt straw hair and his sweatshirt and
his sullen expression—like, why are they putting me through this?
Again?

Her client started to say something, but she shushed him and
said, "Not here. You can never tell who's listening." She glared at
Hack in suspicion. The runt followed her lead and glared too. Hack
beamed back at both.

At the twelfth floor, Hack exited the elevator into the hallway,
leaving the lawyer and her client to their joint hopefully miserable
destiny. Small surveillance cameras hung high from the corners of

55

the walls. There were two courtrooms on the floor, one on the right and one on the left. He took a left.

Two sheriff's deputies stood by a table in front of the courtroom door, obviously extra security for the Kadlec trial. Hack dumped his keys and coins and his phone out on a tray and flashed the deputies the pass Sam had given him. He passed through the electronic sensor booth and retrieved his phone and keys and change and passed into the courtroom.

The courtroom was a small one. The walls were beige. In the back were two rows of chairs with push down plush seats. A low divider with a swinging gate separated spectators from the trial arena in the front. Hack took the last empty seat on the back right.

The prosecutor held center stage. She was a solid black woman in a severe dark suit and an almost buzzcut Afro.

The judge was a thin balding white man in wire-rimmed glasses who stared down on the proceedings from a lordly perch fronted with tawny brown faux-wood panels. His name plate read, "J. Carlson." A couple of anxious female clerks hovered nearby to wait on the judge's demands. An expressionless Court Reporter sat at his little table keying everything everybody said as if none of it mattered to him, which it probably didn't.

Sam and Rick Kadlec sat at a little table on the left facing front. On the right, two additional prosecutors or helpers sat at an identical table with laptops in front of them. Briefcases and boxes with documents spilled out over both tables. There was no laptop on Sam's table, just one thick black three-ring notebook.

It took only a couple of minutes for Hack to catch up. The prosecutor was a Ms. Johnson. Ms. Johnson was devoting her morning to pummeling Sam and his client with the gory details of Kadlec's crime.

Her current witness was a florid faced man in a black suit. He had buckled up his pants almost to his armpits, a maneuver by which he announced to the world not only that he was fat but that he knew it. He wore a white dress shirt with a collar two sizes too small. He had left his collar unbuttoned, but his Adam's apple bulged out anyway over the green knot of his knit tie.

The night before, Sam had explained over the phone what he wanted from Hack. "At a football game, most people follow the ball around, from quarterback to running backs or pass receivers or whoever. Some smart football people say to ignore the ball and watch the linemen. Line play is where the game is decided."

"I know what you mean," Hack said. "In a Twins game, the TV camera follows the ball. But when I go in person, I can see the whole field. Sometimes for fun I focus on the middle infielders or watch the outfielders to see where they position themselves before each pitch."

"Exactly," Sam said. "I need to know what's going on across the whole field. I'll handle the prosecutor and the witnesses and the exhibits and, with luck, the judge. You do me a favor and observe the jurors. Later tell me anything you notice about them. In this trial, the game will be decided in their minds."

"I'm not a mind reader."

"Pick up whatever you can."

The witness's name turned out to be Dr. Badler. He was an expert on explosives. He was explaining the use of black powder.

Badler explained, "Although of course it is not a recent innovation, in fact, black powder can be very destructive."

"Is that why the Boston Marathon bombers used black powder in their pressure-cooker bombs?"

Sam shot up and said, "Objection!"

The judge said, "Sustained."

The prosecutor nodded at Judge Carlson as if she were pleased with his ruling, then turned back to her witness.

Johnson: What is the most common explosive used in pipe bombs in the U.S.?

Badler: Black powder.

Johnson: What is black powder?

Badler: It is the original form of gunpowder invented in ancient China. Europeans improved on it during the Middle Ages many centuries ago. It is basically an explosive mixture of potassium nitrate or sodium nitrate, plus charcoal and sulfur.

Johnson: What licensing requirements exist for the purchase of black powder?

Badler: None.

Johnson: What background checks are required to purchase black powder?

Badler: None.

Johnson: What licensing is required to sell black powder?

Badler: None.

Johnson: What licensing requirements exist for the purchase of black powder?

Badler: None.

Johnson: What background checks are required to purchase black powder?

Badler: None.

Johnson: Are sellers required to conduct background checks?

Badler: No.

Johnson: What records are sellers of black power required to keep of their sales?

Badler: None.

Johnson: What in your experience is the amount of black powder required to make a bomb?

Badler: Three pounds of black powder will make a lethal pressure cooker bomb.

Johnson: You know that how?

Badler: It is generally accepted within the scientific community. And from experience, from hundreds of cases I have personally examined.

Johnson: What is the current limit on purchase of black powder?

Badler: Fifty pounds.

The prosecutor spouted what Hack recognized as formulaic language to get an exhibit admitted into evidence. Sam did not object.

A screen hung on a side wall opposite the jury. A woman at the prosecutor's table clicked a button. On the screen flashed a photo of a pile of twisted black metal. Hack recognized part of the steering wheel and the bent frame of the roof but not much else.

The prosecutor quickly established that the photos showed Penn Lajoie's post-bombing Humvee and that the witness Badler had examined it personally. A series of photos showed the devastated vicinity around the Humvee from all angles. Debris lay everywhere. Hack thought he spotted part of a human thigh on the ground, still in its pants leg.

She asked, "What happened to Penn Lajoie when the bomb exploded?"

Sam objected that the expert was not a medical doctor, but after some wrangling, Judge Carlson allowed Badler to testify as to the physical effects of explosives on the human body in general.

Dr. Badler looked at the jury as he spoke. "Because of the location of the bomb under him, Professor Lajoie was in the bomb's blast radius. A powerful shockwave slammed into him. The human body is like a gelatin, or a sack of water. As the shock wave passes through a mostly liquid human body it ruptures his organs and everything else inside him. In a single instant, it shakes him to death."

"Was there more?" Johnson asked.

"There was the shrapnel. The explosion converted pieces of the automobile into hundreds of projectiles, chunks of metal that eviscerated him and tore him to pieces."

"Did the bomb cause other consequences?"

"The bomb led to a fire from the vehicle's fuel, which charred and ultimately destroyed most of Professor Lajoie's remains."

The prosecutor nodded and her associate clicked again to show a slide of the black tube a few feet long.

"Sir, who is that?"

"That is, or was, Penn Lajoie."

Recalling the role Sam had asked him to play, Hack was happy to take his eyes off the photos and try to read the jury's reactions.

Different jurors wore different expressions. Some looked disgusted, some horrified, some sad. A middle-aged white woman with a bowl haircut and bangs looked very sad. One older Asian man was silently crying.

One juror was different. He was white man in his mid-twenties, with a dark man bun and a neat black goatee. He sat erect, with perfect posture. He was slender, with a thin face and a thin nose. His expression looked more inquisitive than disapproving. Hack experienced a flash of intuition that he was someone Sam might want on Rick Kadlec's jury.

Johnson: As part of your preparation for this testimony, did you have occasion to examine the basement of defendant Rick Kadlec's house?

Badler: Yes.

Johnson: What did you find?

Badler: Among other things, a supply of black powder and a small factory for its manufacture, including the manufacture of its ingredients.

Johnson: What are the ingredients of black powder?

Badler: Primarily saltpeter, sulfur and charcoal.

Johnson: Did the basement contain any of these ingredients?

Badler: All.

Johnson: Were you able to determine the defendant's source for the ingredients?

Badler: Yes.

Johnson: What was the source of the defendant's saltpeter?

Badler: He made it himself.

Johnson: Please explain.

Badler: He made it from urine.

Johnson: Is that unusual?

Badler: Very. It is the hardest way.

Johnson: Were you able to determine how the defendant did that?

Badler: To start with, he filled a drum with manure.

Johnson: Whose manure?

Sam (rising): Objection!

Judge Carlson (to Ms. Johnson): Counselor, unless you wish to take the trial down paths best left unvisited, why don't we just say "manure" and leave it at that?

Johnson: Yes, your honor. (To the witness). How did he use the manure, regardless of source?

Badler: He had a 55-gallon drum nearly full of it. At the bottom he had placed a filter and valve and a drain with trays.

Johnson: Then what?

Badler: Then he urinated into it—

Sam: Objection!

Judge Carlson (to both lawyers): May we stipulate that this was someone's urine without at this time attempting to determine whose? Unless the witness can identify to a reasonable degree of scientific certainty where the urine came from?

Sam: We're willing, Your Honor.

Johnson (to the witness): Please proceed, Dr. Badler.

Badler: After placing human urine in the drum, urine from—

Johnson: From someone—

Badler: From someone—was repeatedly deposited into it in relatively small quantities. Then he poured water on top of the urine. At some point, he would open the valve and allow liquid to flow onto the trays at the bottom. Then he allowed the liquid on the trays to dry out. The dry residue was saltpeter, which he mixed with charcoal and sulfur easily purchased from a garden store to make his gunpowder.

Johnson: How long is it required to leave the ingredients to marinate, as it were, in the barrel?

Badler: At least ten months.

Johnson: Were you able to infer anything about the defendant's state of mind from this process?

Sam (rising): Objection!

Johnson: The issue of premeditation is obviously relevant, Your Honor.

Judge Carlson: Save that characterization for the end of the trial, Counselor. Sustained. The jury will disregard the Prosecution's use of the word "premeditation."

Hack had been watching the jurors. Their faces registered about the same as before, most of them disgusted or repulsed, except for young Mr. Manbun, who revealed only a cool detached curiosity.

Johnson: Have you in your experience encountered other instances of people manufacturing their own saltpeter?

Badler: More than one would expect, given that it is very easy to obtain readymade.

Johnson: How would one do that?

Badler: You can buy it easily online, in bottles and bags. And get next-day delivery. It's sold in garden stores, sometime under the name "stump remover."

Johnson: In your experience, why do some bombers make their own saltpeter rather than buy it?

Sam objected again and there was some more wrangling, but Badler continued.

Badler: Obviously for purposes of secrecy. Online transactions require credit cards, which leave a trail. Stores have clerks who remember customers. Many stores have surveillance cameras that record who comes and goes. That happened in the case of the Boston Marathon bombers when they bought readymade gunpowder at a fireworks store.

Johnson: Earlier, you testified that the legal limit for purchase of black powder is fifty pounds?

Badler: That is correct.

Prosecution: Returning to your examination of the remains of the vehicle, are you able to provide an estimate with reasonable scientific certainty as to how much black powder was used in the bomb that killed Penn Lajoie?

Badler: Yes.

Prosecution: How did you make that estimate?

Badler: (a technical explanation whose terminology Hack couldn't follow).

Johnson: How much black powder was used in the bomb that killed Penn Lajoie?

Badler; At least 100 pounds of black powder.

Johnson: More than the fifty pounds that is the legal limit on purchases?

Badler: More than twice as much.

11 The Annals of Internal GC Struggle

"Beethoven music is rape music. When I hear this man's AGGRESSION, my hands shake, my eyes tear up, and my SPIRIT trembles, as his orgiastic climaxes tear apart my insides!"

Gaea Free, *Annals of Internal GC Struggle*

Back home that afternoon, Hack brewed a big pot of coffee and poured a big mugful and set it next to his laptop on the kitchen table. He sat down in front of them.

He had the house to himself. Mattie was out on one of the random shifts she'd been taking as a waitress at Berringer's.

Thanks to Calvin, Hack also now had someone new to search for: "Gaea Free." He'd seen no such name in Sam's case files. Hack had sent an encrypted email to Sam to ask Kadlec about Gaea Free, but Hack already knew Kadlec wasn't going to tell Sam anything.

Hack found nothing about any person named Gaea Free on the "surface" web—a term for the regular Internet used by most people—regardless whether Hack spelled the name "Gaea or Gaia" or "Free" or "Freigh" or any other variant.

Hack ducked back into the GC system and as he expected found no Gaea Free there either.

But also thanks to Calvin, Hack could now search on the Darknet. Darknet websites didn't have catchy or easily remembered names. Their names were just long random strings of characters. And the string from Calvin which Hack had saved on his phone turned out to identify a private discussion group on the Darknet. That location plus the password from Calvin got Hack into something entitled *The Annals of Internal GC Struggle.*

Reading the *Annals*, Hack felt as if he had stumbled into one of those Dostoevsky novels they had assigned him in school. There were at least three: *The Possessed* and *The Demons*, and *The Devils*. Or were those all just different names for same one? Whatever; in them (or it), a bunch of radicals thought and talked themselves into an intellectual circle jerk and wound up murdering one of their own.

It turned out these GC employees had formed their internal GC group even before GC fired Hack. Hack's investigation became a weird version of déjà vu: after the fact and from the outside, Hack was now looking deep inside the GC workings that cost him his career.

As he read, Hack had to remind himself one more time—he kept having to do this—he was not the center of the world. He had just been collateral damage, an innocent almost-bystander, a random individual standing in the line of fire, a person of no consequence to important people who had taken upon themselves the all-encompassing aspiration of saving the earth and redirecting the entire future course of all humanity in its necessary and inevitable transition towards Utopia.

Hack found too much material in the *Annals* to dump on Sam, especially in the middle of trial. Hack summarized what he had time to read in an eighty-three-page memo it took him sixteen hours to write.

At some point, he was vaguely aware that Mattie came in and laid her strong soft hands briefly on his tense shoulders and kissed his neck and disappeared.

He knew he was going to have to drive into Minneapolis to see Sam in person early in the morning, but when he finally stood up from his chair it was three AM. His back ached. He visited the head and lay down next to Mattie in their bed and set the alarm for two hours of sleep.

12 Hack Reports To Sam

"Plant breeding is rape. What is rape but the insertion of genetic material without the recipient's CONSENT? When did any corn plant or fruit blossom consent to any human penetrating its pistil with a long tool? NEVER!"

Gaea Free, *Annals of Internal GC Struggle*

7:30 AM in Sam's office. Across the expanse of the wide ebony desk, Hack handed his memo to Sam and leaned back in his visitor's chair.

Sam leafed through the thick sheaf of pages. "You could have just emailed me or drop-boxed this monstrosity."

"I'm getting paranoid. There are too many people out there with skills like mine. This is definitely confidential."

"If I read it, what will I read?"

"Extracts from what I've found so far in *The Annals of Internal GC Struggle.*

Sam arched his right eyebrow. "Which are?"

"A secret discussion group on the Darknet, where some of the loonies who work for GC go to hash out their crackpot theories of social transformation."

"You sound kind of judgy."

"Read my memo and you'll get pretty judgy yourself."

Sam asked, "Why should I care about any of this?"

"You wanted to know everything your boy Kadlec was involved in," Hack said.

Sam asked, "Did you find me some alternate suspects? My Real Killer?"

"Hard to say right now. Maybe oodles, maybe none."

"How long is this memo?"

"Eighty-three pages."

Sam leaned back in his swivel chair and folded his hands in his lap. He relaxed into an uncharacteristic quiet posture, both intense and intent, divesting himself of his usual restless movement. He stared up in the direction of Bea's photo on the wall, as if pointing his right ear at Hack. He was going to listen. He said, "Tell me."

"All eighty-three pages?"

Sam glanced at his watch. "You woke up at six AM for nothing. Court was postponed. I've got all day. Hit the high points and then I'll read the whole thing myself."

"It's complicated."

"I've litigated elections. I'm used to complicated."

"You asked for it," Hack said, "GC claims its business model means the company doesn't need to track user searches. It rakes in its profits other ways. That's their marketing pitch, and it's a good one. Users are getting more sensitive all the time about having their Internet use tracked."

"Understood."

"But there's a but."

"When isn't there?"

"But," Hack said, "Regardless whether GC's claim about not needing to track people is true, there's no technical obstacle to GC tracking users all they want. And GC employees have been doing that."

"Why?"

"All sorts of reasons, mostly political. Employees were complaining. They didn't like where the searches were taking customers, to troublemaking climate deniers like Penn Lajoie and to websites and political candidates the employees hate, and so on. And then, when GC grew explosively, GC brought in a lot of new employees, fresh from the campus, bringing in with them a lot of social justice theories they were itching to act out in the real world."

Sam kept his dark eyes steady on Bea's photo, right ear pointed at Hack.

Hack went on. "GC culture radicalized. Sometimes the radicals wandered in on their own, sometimes new people absorbed the radicalism from others already there, and there was even a group called the Democratic Communists of America which intentionally infiltrated."

"Infiltrated?"

"Their word, not mine," Hack said. "To appease their employees, GC put together something they called a 'Justice Team' to monitor search results. This Justice Team went off on its own and changed its name to 'Consciousness Team'."

Sam asked, "And Rick was part of this Consciousness Team?"

"Right," Hack said. "To work out a program and to hash out differences of opinion, the Consciousness Team formed a private discussion group on the Darknet. They made a record of their discussions. It's called *The Annals of Internal GC Struggle.*

"Sounds important."

"Self-important, I think. And consistent with what you'll read in my memo."

"What kind of differences did they need to hash out?"

"They all agree that technology is destroying the earth and humans are responsible and time is running out and it's a crime to have babies in a world like this."

Sam nodded. "Makes sense."

"It does?"

Sam said, "Sure. And since it's wrong to have babies, it follows logically that sex that leads to babies is wrong too, and then even having the type of sex people have when they want to have babies is suspect. And I bet they split into bunch of factions, right?"

"Right," Hack said.

"And then the factions got more and more extreme, right?"

"Right again," Hack said. "Every faction had to distinguish itself from the others. I guess the easiest way to do that is to outdo the others by staking out more extreme positions."

"To be heard above the noise," Sam said.

"Sounds right," Hack said. "And everything got personal. Friendships broke down. Everybody kept raising the stakes."

Sam said, "And I'm guessing the stakes weren't just who'd win the faction fights. They included status in the company, flattering attaperson memos, plum promotions, not to mention bigger salaries and stock options. Faction decides who gets what."

"I don't know about that."

"Take my word for it," Sam said.

"I guess you've seen this kind of thing before, haven't you?"

"Student days," Sam said. "And friends trapped in academia. Where does Rick Kadlec fit in?"

"The *Annals* are a mudhole of rage and hate. And your boy Rick is right there in full wallow."

"Which faction?"

"Just monitoring people didn't change anything. The factions got more and more frustrated. They wanted action. In Rick's case, that meant what anarchists call 'direct action'. Blowing things up. And blowing people up too. He spells it out in one document he wrote, *The Man and The Mask.*"

Sam sorted through Hack's memo until he found his client Rick's article. "He wrote this?"

13 The Man and the Mask

From *The Annals of Internal GC Struggle,* By Rick Kadlec

"Remember, remember,
The Fifth of November
Gunpowder treason and plot.
I see no reason
Why gunpowder treason
Should ever be forgot.

Guy Fawkes, Guy Fawkes, 'twas his intent
To blow up the King and the Parliament.
Three score barrels of powder below
Poor old England to overthrow."

English Nursery Rhyme

How long are we going to sit like teenagers in our cubicles and stroke our keyboards and our genitals?

The time for monitoring is past. The time for complaining is past. Technology is destroying our planet. We're on the verge of extinction. It's time for action. We can set the example by taking direct action. By any means necessary.

Some of you have criticized me for saying "by any means necessary." You don't get my point. By means that are "necessary," I don't mean just any means at all. I mean we should use only means that will not themselves also contribute to the ongoing destruction of our planet.

After all, if we use their weapons, we become them. We cannot use modern technology to remove the blight of modern technology. We must use pre-modern technology. Then, we will show by example that pre-modern technology can be just as effective as modern technology and in fact can defeat it if we act in the right spirit and state of consciousness. Then the masses will be more willing to abandon other modern technology, don't you see?

We must become low tech killers.

No automatic rifles. No plastic explosives. Even smokeless powder is an invention of nineteenth century white supremacists. We must use only locally sourced original formula gunpowder, "black powder," whose inventors were Chinese and not Europeans—not white people.

We all want freedom. Anarchy is freedom. Anarchy means no state violence, no coercion. But technology enables coercion.

Ideas are bulletproof. Did you know that before the original Guy Fawkes was hung, he jumped off the gallows and killed himself? That was freedom too. Freedom to die by his own hand, not by the hand of Authority.

Remember that time we all got together at my place and we all put on our masks and watched *V for Vendetta*? Gaea and Calvin and Thalassa and I and the other comrades, all together, enjoying the inspiration, the insight, the example?

I miss those times.

Remember that scene in the movie, where everyone in the mob is wearing the Guy Fawkes mask, and Guy Fawkes escapes? That togetherness, that's what I miss.

You see? We become a collective being, in which no individual maintains any individual being separate from anybody else. That way we can rebel. We can defeat the oppressor.

El pueblo unido jamás será vencido. The people united will never be defeated.

Gaea, don't you see? It's only together we are powerful. We can make a difference. I can make a difference. Together we make a difference. You and I.

Remember, God is in the rain.

To which someone going by the name "VOR" had posted a comment:

"Do you get all your history from movies? The real Guy Fawkes was no anarchist. He wanted to blow up the Protestant king because he wanted a Catholic king. And what if, in your future anti-tech anarchist utopia of freedom, some free person decides to exercise all that freedom by making smokeless powder and selling it? How will you stop this person without coercion? Who will do the coercing? The anarchist state? You make no sense. You do know that, don't you?"

14 Some Real Killers For Sam

"Jane Austen novels are rape. ALL she writes about is MARRIAGE. What is marriage but the consecration patriarchal society CASTS over heterosex? What is heterosex but RAPE?"

Gaea Free, *Annals of Internal GC Struggle*

Sam dropped Hack's memo onto his desk and asked, "Who was in the Guy Fawkes Battalion besides Rick?"

"No one I found," Hack said. "As far as I can tell, he was the entire Battalion all by himself."

"So where are my alternate suspects? My real killers?"

"First, let me explain the factions a little. I give capsule descriptions on Page 12."

Sam flipped through pages and stopped and read for a minute. He looked up at Hack.

Hack explained, "Nobody else thought Rick went far enough. The first faction to split from the Guy Fawkes Battalion collected under the name 'Lithies'. Rick originally coined the Lithies nickname as an insult, but as happens a lot with these groups, the Lithies reacted by taking the nickname proudly as their own."

"Lithies? What's that?" Sam asked.

"Lithie comes from a Greek word for "stone." As in stone age. Lithies reject all metal tools as the original fatal compromise with technology which started humanity down the road to our imminent ruin. Lithies see the Guy Fawkes group as traitors to Mother Earth."

Hack went on. "Then the Lithies themselves split into three factions: the Paleos, the Mesos and the Neos, corresponding to the three stages archaeologists use to label human prehistory: Paleolithic, in which small groups of humans lived by hunting and gathering; Neolithic, in which humans gathered in settled communities to farm, and the Mesos, somewhere in between. All of them use only stone, bone and wood tools."

Sam said nothing.

"All factions reject modern technology. They just fight over how modern the technology has to be for them to reject it."

Sam stared at Hack with an expression Hack couldn't read. Sorrow? Disgust? Misery?

Hack said, "Anyway,"

"Anyway," Sam agreed.

Hack continued. "The Neos are all women. They are feminists and vegetarians. They reject all patriarchy. They consider eating meat a male activity and embrace farming to raise grain and vegetables.

"The Neo leader is a woman calling herself Gaea Free. Gaea is a Greek name for the earth mother goddess. She has a comrade who calls herself Thalassa Free. I had to look that one up. Thalassa is the name for Gaea's sister goddess, the ocean. You can read Thalassa on Page 24. Ignore her grammar; she's sure grammar is sexist.

"And in my memo, I put two of Gaea's posts right after the one by Thalassa. Enjoy,"

15 Real Killer 1: Neo Thalassa Free

From *The Annals of Internal GC Struggle,* By Thalassa Free

Am I the only one noticed that the Guy Fawkes Battalion is a guy? It's even named after a "guy." Tells you everything. A Guy rebellion not a rebellion against violence. It more the same old white guy male violence.

Guy Fawkes Battalion violence will be mechanical and oppressive, and not organic and intimate as female violence is. What we need more female violence, not male violence.

Say "Neo" if you like. We proud take that name for our own. We proud live as our foremothers lived long ago, before male greed for copper led men to gouge out and scar our Mother Earth Gaea, to build their infernal blast furnaces, to torture Gaea's flesh into metal weapons of war.

We will live as women and only as women.

We will farm. We will eat what we grow. We will be the Matriarchy.

We will farm. We will use the wheel, the millstone, the loom, the pot and the oven. Those are proper Neo.

We will farm. No mines. No metal. No blast furnaces. No meat from kill animals for flesh. Like flesh of Gaea. Disgusting.

We are the Mother. The Earth Mother. But the Earth will be our only Mother. We will not be mothers no more. To be a mother to be raped, and we will not be raped no more.

We reject all male domination, patriarchy, of male violence, and we will banish the devil technology those forms oppression brought into the world.

We will farm. We will hunt no animal and we will use no metal. We will not make war, the male thing.

We will not aggress, we will cooperate.

We will share our feelings, all of them.

We will be hysterical and it will be good!

75

We will not suppress our feelings. Any of them, for they are all legitimate, they all matter, they all *count*, goddammit!

And we count too!

To which "VOR" had posted this comment:

"If you want to live Neolithic, why are you writing? Writing came in about the same time as metal. Do you know anything about history at all?"

16 Real Killer 2: Neo Gaea Free

From *The Annals of Internal GC Struggle,* By Gaea Free

There are a lot of really male IDEAS in these *Annals.* And male people too.

Mostly sellouts, DESERTERS, paid agents for Big Energy, turncoats, renegades, spies, squealers, snitches, and TRAITORS to our Mother Earth.

That's what I read all the time.

And I don't just mean VOR. Oh, he's bad enough. He deserves whatever he gets. But others. The other males. I am SICK of them.

Does the Guy Fawkes Battalion guy think medieval technology is okay? Metal swords and knives? Big bombs? Pottery wheels?

And Calvin with his meat. KILLING creatures. Munching their flesh. Disgusting.

And what is old Middle Mel the Meso Man up to? Sometimes compromise is treason all by itself. But that's just like the toxic male he is. Looking for a way to lie and play male mind games and duck around the truth.

I am down with HYSTERIA, and it is good.

17 Culture Work: The Correct Path

From *The Annals of Internal GC Struggle*, by Gaea Free

I have read so much in our *Annals* about movies and books and video games with revulsion and disgust. So many GCers WHO SHOULD KNOW BETTER internalize and actualize colonialist, white supremacist and cisnormative patterns of thought, leading them to male supremacist modes of discourse that have oppressed and committed violence against women for millennia.

We MUST ALL OF US work together towards a future when people with revolutionary consciousness control culture, which movies are made, what games people enjoy playing, which JOKES people are permitted to laugh at.

We must intervene in the culture and help shape it. We do that and we develop our skills at recognizing and eliminating toxic ideas. We do that and we wreck OBSTACLES to our ultimate success in transforming the world.

But we MUST recognize that for the time being, some people still resent being told what is best for them. They are offended by the idea other people know better than they do what to be permitted to enjoy.

Considering that we are the people who really do know better, what is to be done?

We INTERVENE.

But as one young GCer asked me, "What does it mean to intervene?"

I answered, "Write. Write and call. Post and tweet and review. Friend and unfriend. Get YOURSELF in a position as a critic on a website. If you need to, get together with your comrades and build your own website. If you cannot do that, then comment. If need be, TROLL. But do not remain silent!"

The same young GCer asked me, "But my parents want me out of the house. Even my mother. How can I find time for culture work and make a living at the same time? That is asking a lot. I only have so much time and energy, and I have a lot of issues to work through."

I answered, "Get a Civil Service job. The demands are few and the rewards are many. Civil Service workers enjoy wonderful job security. Once in, you're almost IMPOSSIBLE to fire. Civil Service rules and unions will also protect you from the irritating demands of some bosses. Light work duties will provide you plenty of TIME for culture work, even DURING working hours. And there is a very good chance you will have a supportive BOSS, especially at a state-run university."

But my real purpose in this post is to help you intervene more effectively, regardless whether it's from Mom's basement or Uncle Sam's cubicle.

Here are some principles I have learned from my own activism:

Principle 1: Don't label yourself or tip your hand.

You see a movie. The movie normalizes white supremacy. Now what?

Just labeling it may warn your comrades among the woke, whose awareness enables them to see white SUPREMACY for what it is.

But what about those NOT YET aware as you and your comrades? Don't you want to bring them along?

If you just label a movie sexist, white supremacist, racist, homophobic, transphobic, Islamophobic, no matter how right you are, the sad fact is that many will just tune you out. And these are the people you should be trying to REACH. They will regard you as just another so-called "SJW" fanatic. You may feel better, but you won't convince anybody except those who already agree with us.

Worse, you may wind up appealing to the rebellious streak in less developed people, who resent being told they are racist or sexist, especially when it is TRUE. You wind up stimulating more interest in the movie.

Principle 2: Use The Language of Traditional Criteria.

You can better maintain your credibility as a critic or commenter by impersonating a politically neutral stance, even though we all know there is no such thing.

How? By your choice of the CRITERIA you talk about.

Instead of OUR terminology, use THEIRS, by which I mean the language of "traditional" movie critics who care about plot, dialogue, character development and all the other supposedly "value-free" terminology that has masked underlying white male cisnormative supremacy so effectively over the centuries. You may need to hold your NOSE, but you be much more convincing and effective.

For example, if some movie presents a white supremacist version of history, don't say "white supremacist," say "confused" or "unconvincing."

If some stalwart heterosexual white male is presented positively, for example, as a white man who did something NOBLE for people of color, the most effective tactic may not be to deny the events ever happened. People believe what they see happen in films. You can discredit the white man and his whiteness more effectively by attributing his conduct to his "white savior complex," implying that his motives were racist, even if and ESPECIALLY IF he doesn't know they were racist. You can thereby discredit not only the act but the PERSON who performed the act—killing two birds with one stone, as Calvin the Paleo might say if he talked better.

Likewise, it may be effective to say the movie was "grossly oversimplified" and leave it at that. Here are other examples of useful words and phrases:

- "Safe"
- "Lazy"
- "Simple-minded"

- "Paint-by-the-numbers"
- "Cartoon patriotism" (like there is some other kind)
- "Demonizes (here fill in the name of a victim group)"
- "Heavy-handed."

The other day I read a book review I really admired. A socially aware critic wrote "what the book tries to say is not as interesting as what it reveals about whiteness."

Perfect: inscrutable yet negative. And the ally who wrote it was a white guy.

Of course, don't COPY from my list above. These are just examples. Think of your own, as long as they don't transgress diversity and inclusivity justice principles, of course. You'll be more convincing.

Principle 3: Who Made This?

For cinema, you can also discredit almost any film by pointing up the implicit bias rooted in the identity of the author, director, cast member, or even technical staff like gaffers and "best boys"—a sexist term if there ever was one.

What does a white man know about being black? Or a cisgender know about being trans?

In these cases, the filmmakers are trespassing on others' turf. They deserve all the contempt you can level at them.

But don't hit the wrong targets. By the same logic, take note when the problematic film contains work by someone not themselves problematic. Example: "[name of African-American actress here] did good work. She just couldn't save the otherwise botched film."

That kind of thing.

Conclusion:

We should be flooding websites and social media with our reviews, attacks and plugs. Favor entertainment with kickass feminist superheroes. Slam any that smack of patriarchy or white supremacy.

You ask, what if the white person is an ALLY? Remember, it is ALWAYS the oppressed who take the lead in opposing oppression. The days of the white male heteronormative savior are over.

Bonus: I personally know some activists whose culture WORK has led them to other greater things. One comrade got a high paying job designing feminist video games. Another is now writing greenlighting and shooting down transgender movie scripts. I myself am exploring a position involving proposed projects for a major studio. Something to motivate you!

18 The Way of the Paleo

"So much of left-wing thought is a kind of playing with fire by people who don't even know that fire is hot."

George Orwell

Sam said, "Do you think I can make a case that one of these Neo women killed Penn Lajoie?"

"Going to be tough," Hack said. "Not if they're consistent. The technology of the bomb that killed Lajoie goes against what they claim they believe. The black powder, the metal, everything. Those are things that stone age people didn't have yet."

Hack paused, then added a thought. "Although I could see Thalassa or Gaea killing someone else sometime—they seem angry enough."

"That does me no good," Sam said. "How about the Paleos?"

"I think a Paleo would be an even bigger stretch. If anything, a Paleo is even less likely to make a bomb. Paleos believe we must live as our oldest human ancestors evolved on the African Savannah, hunting and gathering in small groups."

"Did you find any?"

Hack said, "The most outspoken Paleo was a man named Calvin Bagwell. I knew him when I worked at GC. He is currently trying to live an authentic paleo life in the jackpine wilderness out past Ojibwa City."

"How do you know that?"

"Gus and I found him and talked to him. He's how I got access to the *Annals* in the first place. He gave me the Darknet address and the password."

Sam said, "So he's in with these others and he may know something about someone else, right? Who might be my Real Killer?"

"Possibly."

"You're going to talk with him again?"

Hack nodded. He had his own reasons for finding Calvin again anyway. "I'll do that. Meanwhile, I put his final post in the *Annals* on page 46."

19 Real Killer 3: Calvin

From *The Annals of Internal GC Struggle,* By Calvin Bagwell

The Guy Fawkes Battalion poses as radical, but he is a sell-out like the others. As Thalassa and Gaea spell out in one of their few progressive posts, Rick continues to accept the technology that led to capitalism and would inevitably lead once again back to capitalism's advanced technology and climate catastrophe.

Sure, he makes a big show pretending to reject technology, for example, that he will use medieval weapons like black powder in his so-called direct action, but so what? He must use technology to make the black powder. Where does he get the ingredients for the powder?

Even if you make your own gunpowder, the only way to make it yourself without visiting a modern store is to use urine. But you have to store the urine for months. In what?

In a metal barrel? Technology.

In clay pottery? Technology.

The mixing? Done by technology.

And where does he plan to get the sulfur? Sulfur comes from mines. Can anyone think of any activity more hateful towards Mother Earth than digging holes in her flesh and gouging out chunks of her flesh?

Neos like Gaea and Thalassa are just as bad. They also pose as radical, but they want to live in settled farming groups. And how will they handle the communicable diseases that come with living in large settled groups? And the sewage? What about that?

Technology.

Pottery? Just another technology. Tearing out the clay despoils and exploits Mother Earth. It is no different from the mining the Guy Fawkes Battalion wants to continue. Traitors.

Farming? More exploitation. Human beings should not be controlling and breeding and exploiting vegetation. Let the plants grow where Mother Earth grows them. Leave Her alone.

The way of the Paleo is altogether different: to respect Mother Earth. To leave no mark. To leave no trail. When I pass by, no one will ever know I was even here. As a fully human Paleo, I will be invisible. They will see only Mother Earth and her bounty, which I will leave unharmed.

I adopt the Way of The Paleo. Not only physically but spiritually and intellectually as well. I commit totally. To be that First Man who once shared the bounty of Mother Earth with all its creatures and now does so again.

A child surrounded by others of my kind, I now walk without my Eve into the Garden.

A who, not a what.

No knowledge of good and evil. No eternal life.

A human animal.

A creature of flesh, flesh of my flesh and bone of my bone.

You will know me no longer. And I will know not you.

Goodbye, Tiff Madden, my once beloved.

Hello, Gaea Free, my true Mother Earth.

I will cleave only to Gaea my true Mother Earth.

Goodbye science.

Goodbye tech.

Goodbye knowledge.

Goodbye.

20 Real Killer 4: Future Sapiens

"Humanity is the center of all that exists. There is no Higher Power above us."

Future Sapiens, *Annals of Internal GC Struggle*

Sam asked, "When you talk to this Calvin, what's he say?"

"He's not very articulate," Hack said. "Along with modern technology, I think he's given up modern syntax and vocabulary."

"You mean, he just grunts and moans? Like in a caveman movie?"

Hack shrugged. "Just about."

Sam said, "I don't see how you're helping me at all. I don't like any of your alternate suspects for my Real Killer. Each one is weaker than the previous one. But you already know that."

"I've got one other possibility," Hack said. "A long shot."

"Who's that?"

"Someone going by the handle 'Future Sapiens'. A wild card."

"A wild card?"

"Doesn't seem to fit in with the others. Very analytical. Cerebral, even. Focuses not on the past, but what's to come."

"Where?"

Hack said, "Check out Page 74."

21 An Immodest Proposal

From *The Annals of Internal GC Struggle,* by Future Sapiens

We have to ask ourselves, what are the precise parameters of what we are trying to accomplish?

We all agree that we need a world with fewer people. The seven billion currently crowding our planet already constitute a burden too great for our poor old Mother Earth to support. She groans under our massive palpitating pustule of greedy flesh. Her earthquakes shake us off. She swamps us with her floods and tsunamis. Her howls of rage we know as hurricanes.

But how many people precisely can she handle? And how do we get there?

These are practical questions to which there are no easy answers. I offer the Consciousness Team these thoughts not as a definitive blueprint or a detailed design document, but only as a starting point for ongoing discussions that may ultimately lead to a specific plan.

If we are serious about our goals, we need to design our proposed upgrade of human society with as much care and detail as we design any upgrade to any system, such as the ones we implement in our daily work at GC.

Here for our consideration is a suggested starting list of goals:

1. To define a technological stasis point ("TSP) at which human material technology will neither regress nor advance in ways harmful to our Mother Earth;

2. To design a sociopolitical mechanism to prevent any technological advance from the TSP once we have achieved it;

3. To define precisely a demographic stasis point ("DSP"), that is, an ideal human population for our earth which can be maintained at the TSP, and which by necessity must be much smaller than all current population growth projections;

88

4. Not only to support the DSP, but also
5. To design a mechanism to reach the DSP. That is, how do we get from here to there?
6. To identify and resolve any human rights complications which might obstruct or distract us as we engage with all the above.

To take just one example, what is the goal population we are after—the DSP?

The world's human population about ten thousand years ago, at the end of the Paleolithic era, was only about 5,000,000 people.

One sound estimate of the world's population at the end of the Neolithic era was about 40,000,000 people.

Thirty years from now, the world's population is expected to reach at least ten billion (10,000,000,000), or about 2,000 times greater than it was just ten thousand years ago.

Suppose hypothetically, we make our goal population the 5,000,000 people the world supported at the end of the Paleolithic era. How do we reach that population level?

Some of us count on some mass extinction event like a devastating epidemic or a nuclear war or the asteroid which killed off the dinosaurs. And we all recognize that climate change will almost certainly take care of most of the problem if we don't take immediate drastic action.

A mass extinction may happen and therefore relieve us of the obligation to take drastic action ourselves. But if it doesn't, then what? What if the human burden on our planet continues to increase exponentially, as it does right now? For example, demographers predict that the population of Africa alone will increase by one billion just in the next thirty years. Overstressed even now as our planet is, can it feed and otherwise support a billion more Africans?

Without a natural mass extinction event, how will all these excess people be removed? By attrition, the way a corporation reduces its work force? But when a private corporation does that, the former employees are still alive. They continue to eat, consume, and generate earth-destroying waste.

In our current situation, what we need is people dying off without new births to replace them. But can that really happen fast enough to save our earth?

China eventually reversed its one-child policy, and even that was originally intended only to hold the population of just one single country down to one billion, not nearly low enough for our purposes.

Is the solution mass starvation, mass murder, biological warfare-style solutions, or involuntary mass birth control? I invite everyone's thoughts.

I also ask everyone to address human rights concerns. We have to ask, how can we as believers and practitioners of social justice, incorporate our human rights concerns into our plans for reducing the plague of humanity?

22 That's It?

"You soy boys will never get it up to make a revolution. Instead of Marx's 'lumpenprolatariat', I classify you as the 'limpenproletariat'."

VOR, *The Annals of Internal GC Struggle*

"This Future Sapiens is a scary one," Sam said, "But the writing is cold and analytic and cerebral. Doesn't sound like someone enraged enough to commit an immediate murder of any particular person."

"But don't we think Lajoie's murder was politically motivated?"

"How do we know that? Maybe the motive was an old fashioned one like jealousy or revenge or money. Maybe it had nothing to do with cultural theories."

"For example?"

"Something personal. Something that would make someone forget all about theory and just go with rage. That would help me a lot."

"Well, there are some personal grudges. But I don't think they involve Penn Lajoie. He wasn't part of the Consciousness Team. The hot grudges were among Team members themselves, like Gaea and Thalassa Free and the others. Which brings us to Mel Untermeyer."

23 Meso: The Middle Course

From *The Annals of Internal GC Struggle,* By Mel Untermeyer

Why so much anger?

The Guy Fawkes Battalion. The Neos. The Paleos. The factions. The splinters. The rage. The hatred.

We started with the same goals, the same ideals, the same aspirations. But what happened?

Can't we find a path between Anarchist and Neo? Between Neo and Paleo?

I think we can. I call it "Meso." The middle course.

People forget the Paleolithic didn't just lead directly to the Neolithic. The Mesolithic era came in between.

People had pottery, but no potter's wheel.

Their tools were still stone, but they were lighter and smaller.

People dressed in textiles, not just fur.

See?

I reject Paleo, but I reject Neo too.

Gaea, you in particular. You seem so angry all the time. We had it so beautiful. What happened? Why can't we connect anymore?

24 *I Accuse*

From the *Annals of Internal GC Struggle*, by Gaea Free

I am not saying this to hurt anyone, only to help. I read Thalassa's story of the sexual assault she SUFFERED and my heart goes out to her and I am glad she is getting the ATTENTION she needs and deserves. It reminded me how much I need and deserve attention for what has happened to ME, too. I'm suffering too. I'm BURNING up inside, with shame and so many other emotions I cannot even define.

I had my own experience with an ABUSIVE relationship. It started right after I joined GC. He was a higher up. Needless to say, that relationship didn't work out and I barely escaped with my mental health intact and that's when I met Mel.

I told him about what had happened to me, and in the beginning, he seemed kind and supportive. I see now that, with that instinct exploitative MEN like Mel possess, he sensed how vulnerable I was.

It seemed like a DREAM come true: a man who was tender and caring and focused on my needs instead of his own.

But then he wanted us to spend ALL our time together. Eventually I figured out all he really wanted was to separate me off from everyone else in my life so that I would be dependent on him for all my support and especially my self-esteem, which he insidiously tore down at every opportunity.

For example, once he asked me why I had stayed in that previous relationship so long if it were so abusive, as if I had a choice. It turned out he didn't understand me after all. I began to INTERNALIZE what he was hinting at and wonder if it was all my fault I had stayed in it.

At work he acted normal and in private he told me how much he loved me and needed me. That was the worst part, because I suspected he didn't love me for real and was just lying the way that first abusive higher up had lied before.

I began to get really frustrated at work. It seemed Mel was getting all this conspicuous work done and grabbing the attention and the CREDIT for his work and I was getting nothing back for the work I was doing at GC and getting nothing from Mel for the effort I was putting into our relationship, which of course, always detracted from the ENERGY I could have devoted to work if he had not exploited me. Just his constant efforts to ISOLATE me and spend all his time with me so that he would be the main thing that mattered in my life.

That's when our relationship turned into a NIGHTMARE. I began to feel angry and defensive all the time. He kept asking me why I was so unhappy, as if there were something wrong with me, but I realized my unhappiness came from my dissatisfaction with him and what I needed that he was failing to give me, which I tried to explain, but he didn't really listen.

One time I tried to explain all this to him, he screamed at me. At least it felt like screaming, although he denied it later. But I'm sure it was screaming. And he CRIED. And it felt violent. And I realized how violent all the sex was in essence, with the domination he could hold over me physically any time he wanted.

When I left for the last time, he BARELY looked at me, like I wasn't real to him and my feelings didn't count for anything.

That's the trouble, isn't it? We can't complain about sexual abuse without feeling that it's somehow our fault. And that's why I'm writing this. Other women need to know about Mel. I don't want any other woman to go through what I went through with Mel. Even years later, I cry whenever I think of him. And I still BURN with SHAME.

To which someone called herself "Diana" had posted a comment: "I had my own very bad experience with Mel. I agree with Gaea that he is exploitative and brutal. He is emotionally distant and indifferent to women's needs."

After which "Olive" had written how after her sexual experience with Mel, "he failed to return my texts and phone calls. It took me a long time with Gaea, Thalassa and Diana, and a lot of self-examination, before I finally understood that Mel had raped me."

On all this, VOR commented "Every disappointing screw isn't a rape," which led to Diana, Olive, Thalassa and Gaea jointly to sign the following:

"We are ANGRY to HYSTERIA . VOR has got to go. He is a rape apologist. He is pro-rape. We are not safe with him around.

"Women must be believed. Those who refuse to believe WE HAVE BEEN RAPED are raping us all over again.

"We must ban VOR from the Consciousness Team. And from GC. We must excise all his theories and his posts from the *Annals.*

"We are not safe. If we are not safe, then neither is VOR. If he does not believe us, if he defends men like Mel, if he defends any rapists at all, he MUST face the consequences."

25 V For Vendetta—the Movie

"Is that all you got?" Sam asked.

"So far," Hack said.

"I don't see how Gaea Free accusing this Mel guy gets me any closer to finding my Real Killer of Penn Lajoie."

"Neither do I," Hack admitted. "But these women are really enraged. I wouldn't want them even to be aware I exist."

"They're enraged at this Mel and this VOR guy, not at Penn Lajoie," Sam said. He sighed. "I'll scan this thesis of yours today. Meanwhile, keep digging."

"Okay." Hack got up to leave.

But Sam said, "One thing more. See what else you can find by this Future Sapiens. I agree with you about him. Future Sapiens is a wild card of some kind. Maybe his analytic way of writing is just a disguise. Maybe he's a serial killer or something like that."

"Desperate, aren't we?" Hack said, and left.

From Sam's office, Hack drove back towards Ojibwa City. Along the way to Gus's place, he picked up a *V for Vendetta* DVD from a rental box at an Ojibwa City convenience store. Maybe Rick Kadlec's favorite movie held some clue.

Hack parked in Gus's yard and went in through the kitchen door to the living room. Gus looked up from the couch where he sat with a paperback of the John D. MacDonald novel *A Purple Place For Dying*. Hack remembered the book. Travis McGee witnessed the murder of a widow trying to get her husband's estate. Big challenges for Travis, which he mostly met, of course, with some inevitable regrets mixed in.

Hack turned on Gus's television and DVD player and put in the disk. He said, "I've got a movie for us to watch."

Gus stuck a bookmark in his paperback and laid it on a table. "You going to let me in on why?"

"It's research for Sam. This movie deeply influenced his client Rick Kadlec."

"Which explains why you're watching. Why am I?"

"I treasure your insights."

"You're getting paid for your insights. Am I?"

"I'll bill Sam for your time."

"Okay," Gus said. "Insights for money seems fair."

Hack went into the kitchen and opened a pair of Chumpsters from the fridge and came back and handed one bottle to Gus. They watched the movie.

To Hack it seemed just another superhero plot. An evil fascist government rules England. The evil government's experiment goes awry and endows a young man with special powers. The newly anointed superhero dubs himself "V" and puts on a Guy Fawkes mask and saves a girl from rape. Then he kills a string of evil guys, moving up the villain food chain until he kills the evil fascist dictator, in which noble deed he dies nobly himself. The girl dons the mask and takes over V's role. Inspired by V, the people all put on Guy Fawkes masks together and overthrow the evil government.

Direct action. Propaganda of the Deed. The romantic notion of the revolutionary hero inspiring the masses. And in the movie—as opposed to any History book Hack had ever read—it actually works.

The fascists are the usual suspects: white, fundamentalist Christian, sexist, homophobic, anti-Muslim, and so on. Every cliché ever.

If Rick Kadlec loved this movie, that was just more bad news for Sam.

The movie ended. Hack took the DVD out of the player and replaced it in its case and snapped the case shut. Hack asked, "Well, what are your insights?"

"Reminds me a lot of *Phantom of the Opera*,' Gus said.

"I hadn't thought of that."

"V's got that Guy Fawkes mask to cover his disfigurement, and he hides in his secret lair, and he obviously loves the girl, but he can't have her because of his scars. Like a fatal flaw. So he goes all Lord Byron and sacrifices himself for the freedom of others. Very romantic. Straight out of the *Phantom* movie."

"At least in this movie he doesn't play the organ or sing any of those treacly songs," Hack said.

"Yeah, he just plays those old records instead," Gus said. "Almost as bad."

"I liked those old jazz songs," Hack said.

"I'm more of a rock and country guy," Gus said. "You know that. But basically, the movie's a fantasy for INCELs."

"Insell? What's that?"

"Involuntary celibate. Men who aren't having sex, even though they'd like to. Maybe because they're not conventionally good looking or they're poor or they're socially awkward."

"That describes most single men. Most married ones too."

"And most women too," Gus said. "Nowadays the INCEL men at least have a support group of their own. Which would be okay except that in their support group on the Internet they get in this feedback loop where they stoke each other's frustrations and resentments. They work themselves into rage and jealousy at lucky stiffs like you who get to have sex with real live women. And that makes them dangerous. Maybe even violent."

"Violent towards men who get to have sex?"

"Towards women mostly. After all, a lot of INCELS are weak specimens to begin with. If they weren't, they'd probably be having more sex."

"I never heard of any of this stuff," Hack said. "You got more?"

"Well, the movie also has some cosplay in it," Gus said.

"You're an encyclopedia of words I didn't know."

"That's short for costume play. People dress up and pretend to be other people or even other species."

"Other species? Why?"

"They don't want to be human, I guess."

"Why not?"

"Find it offensive or something. Maybe feel guilty."

"About what?"

"Using the earth? Not sure."

Hack asked, "How does a jackpine savage like you living in the woods learn about these cultural developments?"

"I have a teenage son, remember? LG explains it. He's my informant."

"I didn't know about any of this. Maybe I should get out more."
"No you shouldn't," Gus said.

26 Sam At Trial: The Cop

"I was married by a judge. I should have asked for a jury."

Groucho Marx

Time to check on Sam's trial again. Hack slipped into the Courtroom just as Judge Carlson was about to rule on a dispute between Sam and the Prosecutor Johnson. The jury box was empty. Only staff, lawyers and spectators remained in the courtroom for the arguments.

Judge Carlson shuffled some papers. Looking down at them, he read in a monotone: "The Defendant seeks to argue a necessity defense in this case, his contention being that the threat of imminent climate extinction gave him no choice but to violate the technical requirements of the law."

He shuffled some more. "In Minnesota, a defendant asserting a necessity defense must show four elements. First, that the harm that would have resulted from obeying the law would have significantly exceeded the harm actually caused by breaking the law; second, that there was no legal alternative to breaking the law; third, that the defendant was in danger of imminent physical harm; and fourth, that there was a direct causal connection between breaking the law and preventing the harm."

The Judge looked up. "In the case before us, none of these four elements exist: the only harm that would have resulted from the accused's obeying laws against homicide would have been that the victim Penn Lajoie would have continued to exercise his First Amendment right to say things with which the defendant disagreed. Second, defendant had many legal alternatives to murder. Third, defendant was in no imminent physical danger. Given the results as to the first three elements, the fourth element concerning a causal connection has no application here."

Judge Carlson looked over at a Clerk. "The Court will not allow Defendant to present evidence made relevant only under a theory of necessity. Please bring the jury back in."

It looked like Kadlec was going to have a hard time turning the trial into a forum where he could push his climate catastrophe agenda. Kadlec whispered something to Sam. Sam whispered back. Kadlec's whispering grew animated enough that spectators' heads were swiveling in the two men's direction. As the juror filed in, it was obvious that some of them noticed too.

Although Hack wasn't a lawyer himself, he thought watching Sam's trials was turning him into a knowledgeable fan. He supposed Sam was explaining to Kadlec why the judge wasn't going to let Kadlec propagandize. Hack himself wasn't sure it was a good idea anyway. Wouldn't Kadlec preaching his climate rage just pile on more evidence he had a motive for murder?

When the prosecutor Williams stood to speak, Sam laid a gentle hand on Kadlec's arm. Their whispering stopped. They both turned their attention to the front.

Williams called a new witness, a police detective named Crosetti. He was thickset man in his forties. His graying crewcut accentuated the thickness of his upper back and neck. But his suit was a nice blue weave that fit him well. He wore a natty silver stickpin in his striped rep tie.

After the usual preliminaries, Johnson went to work with her witness.

Williams: When you and the two others of your team arrived at the door to speak with the defendant, what happened?

Detective Crosetti: I rang the doorbell and he answered it.

Williams: Did anything unusual strike you at that time?

Detective Crosetti: Yes.

Williams: Please tell the jury.

Detective Crosetti: He was wearing a costume, including a mask.

Williams: Is it unusual in your experience for people to answer the door wearing costumes and masks?

Detective Crosetti: Unique.

Williams: Please describe the costume.

Detective Crosetti: it included a tall black conical hat, a long black wig, a black cloak and a mask.

Williams: Could you see his face?

Detective Crosetti: No, because of the mask.

Williams: Was anything said?

Detective Crosetti: He said, "I knew you were coming, so I dressed for the occasion."

Williams: What happened then?

Detective Crosetti: I asked if we could come in to talk.

He said that would be fine.

We entered.

I asked him why he was wearing a costume.

He told me I would understand soon enough.

I asked him what that meant.

He said, "Don't you know who V is? Or Guy Fawkes?"

I confessed I didn't. I asked him at least to remove the mask and he did.

We sat down in his living room and the defendant went into great detail for at least thirty minutes about this movie he loves called "V For Vendetta," which is about an anarchist who dresses up in a hat and a cloak and a mask and a wig and then fights against a fascist government in England and kills a lot of fascists and cops.

Williams: Let's hold for moment right there.

Williams brought a hat, mask, cloak and wig out and went through the steps of having Crosetti examine the costume and the signed tags and say that this indeed was the very same costume Kadlec had worn. Williams introduced it as an exhibit without objection from Sam and, one at a time, handed each item to the jury, which passed around and examined the hat and the mask and the black cloak and the long black wig.

Williams: Had you seen this costume before?

Detective Crosetti: Yes. In the course of my investigation, I had viewed the video of the protest at Penn Lajoie's speech. The man Penn Lajoie punched was wearing it.

Hack saw Sam twitch and settle back in his chair, but he didn't rise to object to Crosetti's certainty that Kadlec's costume was the same costume shown in the video of Lajoie's speech. Hack guessed that Sam checked his swing because it was indisputable that Kadlec was in fact the protester Lajoie had punched. Why emphasize that harmful fact by objecting to a detail?

Williams: When you sat down in the living room with the defendant, what was the conversation?
Detective Crosetti: The first thing after that, he said, "I did it."
Williams: Please elaborate.
Detective Crosetti: Well, he said that, which I needed to make more specific, so we turned on the video camera and Mirandized him, you know, I told him he had a right to remain silent and get a lawyer and so on.
Williams went through the steps of introducing the video into evidence. Then she showed it:

Rick Kadlec is sitting on a sofa, still dressed in the conical black hat with the long black wig trailing straight down his neck on three sides. But he's not wearing the mask. The face is clearly his.
A voice Hack recognizes as Crosetti's advising Kadlec about his rights and Kadlec says "Your bourgeois legal crap means nothing to me."
Crosetti says, "Are you waiving your rights?"
Kadlec says, "You bet."
Crosetti asks, "Is there anything you'd like to tell us?"
Kadlec says, "I made the bomb. In fact, I manufactured the bomb myself in my basement. I planted it under the passenger compartment in Penn Lajoie's carbon-spewing gas guzzler. I did it. I killed him. Go ahead and arrest me."
Crosetti asks, "Why did you kill Penn Lajoie?"
Kadlec answers, "Because I wanted to kill him. I planned to kill him. It took me months to plan and get ready."
Crosetti asks, "Even before he punched you?"

Kadlec answers, "His wimpy little fascist punch had nothing to do with it. He's a denier. Deniers are killing the planet. But the government never punishes them. It's run by greedy corporations. So I had to kill him."

"Why did you have to kill him?"

"To set an example. This is what should happen to deniers. It's an emergency, don't you see? I suppose a cop like you can't see. But I think a jury will."

Crosetti asks, "A jury will see what?"

"A jury will see why I did it."

"What if they don't?"

"I'll be out one way or the other in ten years."

"How do you figure that?"

"There's no death penalty in Minnesota," Kadlec says. "In ten years, when the full climate catastrophe hits, and society collapses, the prison walls will collapse too. No problem. I can do ten years easy. And get out. If there's still anything left to get out for."

Crosetti says, "You know, we hear a lot of false confessions. Can you prove you killed Penn Lajoie?"

"Sure," Kadlec says. He stands. The camera follows him as he leads the detectives down to the basement. He proudly displays and explains the bags of sulfur and charcoal, the barrels where he made the saltpeter, his bags full of already manufactured gunpowder, his workbench and bomb making tools, his stacks of anarchist literature, including a pamphlet he wrote himself called "Propaganda of the Deed," and his prized collection of different colored Guy Fawkes masks, including masks whose eyebrows, eyes, mustache and little chin strip beards glow in the dark. He puts one of his masks on for the camera and in a flat voice starts intoning,

"Cut our carbon down to zero,
Got to do it now!
Time for you to be a hero
I will show you how."

And so on.

Hack checked to see how the jury was taking the show. Most were staring. One middle-aged woman was shaking her head and making a "Tch...Tch" sound. An older black guy wore a look of disgust. Young Mr. Manbun slumped in his seat, eyes half shut, as if the video bored him and he was going to nod off any second.

It was only getting worse for Sam and his client. Hack stood and slipped out of the courtroom.

27 This is ZNN: Gynodelphia

"Outside of a dog, a book is a man's best friend. Inside of a dog, it's too dark to read."

Groucho Marx

The screen shows Lauren Goodwell in a bright red parka, hood down and dark hair streaming behind her in the wind. She is a vision of newsy loveliness, standing beside a brown wooden sign on a stick planted in the dirt. On the sign is burned in black capital letters the big word "Gynodelphia."

No frown this time—Lauren's got a grin on her face and a smile in her voice: "Hi. I'm standing outside the village limits of Gynodelphia, an alternative community of, by and for women, here in the rural Northland. Security considerations prevent me from telling you the precise location. I'm here to learn more about the launching of a history-making women's community, one that may just possibly set a new standard for how women live in the future. I'm here to interview one of its founders, Gaea Free."

(Establishing shot of the two women sitting facing each other in wooden chairs in an old-fashioned living room. Next shot: the camera is looking over Lauren Goodwell's shoulder to show Gaea's face. Every so often the camera switches to Lauren as she asks a question and then returns to Gaea for the answer.)

Gaea: First, I want to thank you for respecting our need for safety and acquiescing in our request to bring only women technicians with you. We don't feel safe with men around. You understand.

Lauren: Of course I do. There are no men at all in Gynodelphia?

Gaea: No males whatsoever. We are a free community of women, by women, and for women, women who feel called upon to reject the patriarchy and patriarchal technology. We want to live as our foremothers did, but completely without male influence and the pervasive threat of male violence.

Lauren: How did you come up with the name Gynodelphia?

Gaea: From two Greek words, meaning city of women. Which is what we are.

Lauren: How did Gynodelphia come about?

Gaea: A friend with substantial resources bought and donated the land to a collective entity we created.

Lauren: Who owns this entity and the land?

Gaea: That's a matter of some confidentiality. For now I'll just say we share it together.

Lauren: So Gynodelphia is something like a commune?

Gaea: In the sense that we hold all personal property together and we do all the work together. As our foremothers did.

Lauren: There have been a lot of Utopian and experimental communities in the past. They almost always collapse. What makes this one different? Why should you succeed when so many others have failed?

Gaea: We have learned much from the mistakes of our predecessors. We now have a greater consciousness of how patriarchal patterns of thought can invade and interfere with true community. We are on the constant lookout for male ideas, male ways of thinking, male habits of greed and self-gratification. We gather daily in special sessions to deal with issues of destructive male thinking inherited from the past.

Lauren: Could we observe one of these gatherings?

Gaea *(smiling)*: I would need to discuss that with my sisters first. Safety and privacy are necessary for all of us.

Lauren: But it is safe to say that as leader, one of your duties is to be on the lookout for male habits of thought?

Gaea: We don't use words like "duties." What men might call a duty we call a "blessing." For women, at least for women in touch with our womanhood, it's a blessing to work and share.

Lauren: But you are the leader?

Gaea: We are all leaders. But I am a shaman.

Lauren: Are there other shamans here?

Gaea: No, just me. Well, me and Sister Thalassa Free.

Lauren: You know, a moment ago, I expected you to say "Sha*Woman*" and not "Sha*man*."

Gaea *(laughing again)*: No need for that, Lauren. It's a common misconception. The word 'shaman' comes from the language of the Evenk people of Siberia. The word and its root have nothing to do with maleness or the English word "man." The word "shaman" is permissible.

Lauren: Thanks, that's very informative. How will Gynodelphia provide for itself?

Gaea: We will farm, of course. As our Neolithic foremothers did. After all, it was women who invented farming. There's no reason we can't relearn what our foremothers knew.

Lauren: Women invented farming? I think our viewers would be interested in that.

Gaea: Archaeologists agree. While men were off away from home killing and butchering living creatures, women stayed at home gathering. As they gathered, women came to notice how seeds from one plant can create new plants. Seeing this gave our foremothers an idea. They planted the seeds themselves and gathered where they planted. And that was the beginning of agriculture. And the beginning of the Neolithic area, the new stone age, was when people began to live in settled communities.

Lauren: And now you've been farming yourselves?

Gaea: Not yet, Lauren. We're just getting up and running. But we will. This coming summer.

Lauren: Will your farming be any different from current American farming practices?

Gaea: No pesticides or herbicides. And of course we will shun all genetically modified crops.

Lauren: Even fruit?

Gaea: For instance?

Lauren: Like citrus fruits, you know—oranges, limes, lemons, grapefruit, and so on. The ones bred from the original citron.

Gaea: Citron?

Lauren: You mentioned the word "Neolithic." Could you explain for our viewers what that means?

Gaea: The word "Neolithic" is an archaeological term referring to the new stone age.

Lauren: Is that why your group calls itself "Neos?"

Gaea: Yes. We look back to the time before modern technology began, the male technology that led to centuries of patriarchy and war. We want to live the way our foremothers did, before males and their male technology started us down the path that led to the climate catastrophe we all dread today.

(Just moment, a yellow-brown Yorkshire Terrier hops onto Gaea's lap.)

Lauren: Well, who's this little sweetheart? Isn't she adorable?

Gaea: Our sister Artemis. The newest addition to Gynodelphia. She just turned seven months old. And her silky coat is hypoallergenic, so new worries there. She loves to meet new women.

(Artemis hops off Gaea's lap onto the ground and begins to yap furiously at Lauren and the camera.)

Lauren: Artemis, we're friends!

Gaea: Artemis! Stop that!

(The camera follows Artemis as she continues yapping while she runs in little circles. She stops and rolls onto her back and begins to writhe and wave her paws in the air.)

Lauren: Why is she wearing that little lavender diaper-like cloth?

Gaea: Yesterday, she all of a sudden started bleeding a tiny bit. We're a little concerned. We're not sure what caused it. It can be messy. We don't want it on the furniture.

(Artemis jumps up and charges the camera, yipping and barking.)

(Camera cuts to Lauren once again standing in front of the Gynodelphia sign. She shakes her long hair into the wind):

Lauren *(laughing)*: Well, our little sister Artemis decided we'd gotten all the footage we need, and who are we to argue? Signing off from Gynodelphia, in the wilds of the Northland, this is Lauren Goodwell for ZNN.

28 Calvin Visits Gynodelphia

Night. Cold. Sky black. Snow bright. Snow and moon light.
Calvin slips down the bluff onto the dark path.

Towards love.

Towards Tiff.

Houses. Houses and voices. Women's voices.

Lights in a window. Calvin steps to the window and looks in.
Loud women voices.

Many women. Sitting on the floor or in chairs. Arguing.

Tiff there too. She talks. Other women argue. She argues. Other
women talk. All talk. All cry.

Silent, Calvin watches.

Now a woman stands and leaves. Others leave. Tiff leaves. Now
no one.

Calvin waits. No one comes.

No one comes.

Calvin turns and walks back down the path towards the bluff.
Towards the woods.

Sad.

29 Another Interview With Calvin

"If you think dogs can't count, try putting three dog biscuits in your pocket and then give him only two of them."

Phil Pastoret

It was late in the afternoon the day after they watched the *V For Vendetta* movie. Again Hack and Gus stood peering into Calvin's mineshaft.

Calvin was gone. All he'd left behind were a few scraps of meat and bone. A light new snowfall covered the ash and stone from Calvin's fire.

The temperature was in the twenties, and it was pleasant to go gloveless in the warm sun, but, not knowing where the day might take them, Hack and Gus had worn their backpacks.

Shakey dashed past them into the shaft and sniffed all about before he picked up the deer shank and put his paws over it to hold it down. He began to gnaw with gusto, his eyes rolling white in ecstasy.

"Now what?" Hack asked Gus. Hack looked across the creek into the woods. The snowfall had also filled in Calvin's old footprints. Trailing him was going to be harder this time.

"Might be a job for Shakey." Gus said.

"Will he do that? Track, I mean?"

"His choice," Gus said.

The crack from Shakey breaking the bone between his jaws echoed in the tiny rock shelter. He licked at the exposed pink marrow, eyeing Hack. Message: this bone is mine.

"Shakey!" Hack said. Shakey stopped licking and glared at Hack with suspicion.

"Shakey, find Calvin!" Hack commanded.

Shakey kept both eyes fixed on Hack and went back to his marrow.

"I thought so," Hack said.

"Let him finish his lunch," Gus said.

"Don't you feed him?" Hack asked.

"Plenty. But he's still a growing boy. And have you ever seen a dog turn down food?"

"Could he track across all this snow anyway?"

Gus said, "Sure he can. Underwater too. Any place he wants."

"What if he doesn't want?"

Gus shrugged.

Shakey dropped the bone and tipped his snout upwards and slurped down the last remnant of soft marrow. He swept his pink tongue around his jaws and chops and stood and raced around the shaft and sniffed at the debris.

He sprinted between Gus and Hack and slid his way across the frozen creek into the woods. He began to sniff the ground all about. His path wavered and wandered, but after a few minutes, it seemed to Hack that Shakey's route was centering around a straight line heading deeper into the woods.

Hack said, "You think he's tracking Calvin?"

"Shakey obviously loved the man," Gus said.

"Loved his smell, you mean."

"For him, same thing. But let's see."

The furry whiteness of Shakey's hindquarters disappeared into the white background among the scattered trees.

Luckily, Shakey left his own fresh paw tracks in the snow. Gus and Hack had no trouble following him.

The two men hit a few tough spots where they struggled through snow drifts that slowed them down, but in general they made pretty good time, and after about two hours, they found Calvin—rather, they found Shakey, who had found Calvin.

Shakey was sitting and looking up into a tree at a thick lower limb covered by thick bundles of pine branches. Calvin's bare scrawny legs and fur-shod feet straddled the limb and hung down below.

As Hack and Gus came near, Shakey trotted over and greeted each of them in turn, nuzzling their legs and welcoming their friendly cuffs on his hard narrow skull. Then he went back to his post and looked up at Calvin again.

Calvin's voice came from the limb above. "Wolf here, no deer."

Hack didn't get Calvin's meaning but Gus peered up and said. "Is that supposed to be a deer blind?"

"Hunting," was the answer from Calvin.

Gus asked, "You plan on killing a deer with just a spear?"

"Jump down on deer," Calvin said.

"Has that ever worked?" Gus asked.

"No," Calvin admitted. "Hungry."

Gus said to Hack in a low voice, "I bet that deer bone he had before came off some carcass he scavenged." Then, looking up again, Gus said, "Calvin, come on down, will you? I brought you some meat."

"You did?" Hack asked Gus. "So did I."

"Couldn't let the man starve," Gus said.

In two shakes of a spear Calvin shinnied down and said, "Meat?"

Gus unslung his pack and Hack unslung his pack and each laid out the meat he'd brought. Gus unpacked several chunks of thawed venison he had stored in his freezer after the previous deer hunting season. Hack laid out three free-range wild grouse Hack had gathered from the cooler of a St. Paul specialty store where he'd stopped after dropping Sarai at school.

"I hunted this deer myself," Gus told Calvin.

"Hunt yours?" Calvin asked Hack.

"Not personally, but someone did," Hack said. "It's not from a farm." Guessing that shotguns didn't satisfy paleo hunting standards, Hack didn't mention the holes from the pellets.

Gus asked Calvin, "By your rules, is a fire okay?"

"Tried." Calvin looked mournful. "Hard."

"I'll show you," Gus said.

Wet snow blanketed the ground all around. Hack gathered dry tinder and kindling from the bare black branches of still-standing dead and dying trees. While he did that, Gus cleared a space about three feet square of most of its snow and ice and exposed the hard ground below.

Gus explained to Calvin, "Something to remember. A fire laid right on top of snow will cause a tunnel to form as it burns, trapping the heat and melting the snow. Then the melt will put out the fire."

Calvin nodded.

Gus knelt. "And now we'll put a few thicker sticks directly on the ground to lay a foundation, so our fire will hover a bit above ground."

Hack crouched down next to Gus and his makeshift firepit and laid his tinder on the ground. He started with a few dry oak leaves he had plucked off some branches and some dry bark he'd peeled off a birch trunk. Then, for kindling, he layered over the bark handfuls of dry twigs he had broken off dead branches.

Gus took out a cigarette lighter.

Calvin said, "No."

Gus said, "What?"

"I think a lighter is against his rules," Hack said.

Gus looked a question at Hack. Hack said, "Paleo only, remember?"

Gus shrugged and reached into his pack and took out a small patch of some steel wool and an old cell phone.

Hack said. "That old trick with sparks from the battery?" He shook his head. "Still not paleo."

Gus paused for a moment, then reached in again and took out his magnifying glass.

Hack shook his head again. He couldn't resist smirking.

From under his shaggy brows Gus stared dagger eyes at Hack.

Hack asked, "You going to rub two sticks together?"

Gus said, "Say, Calvin?"

Calvin said, "Yes?"

Gus pointed into a thicket. "I thought I saw a deer pass just behind those trees. Check it out, will you please?"

Calvin grabbed his spear and jumped up and ran over to where Gus pointed.

Quicker than Hack had ever seen Gus draw his Glock, Gus yanked his lighter out and lit the tinder and kindling and fed into the small flames a few progressively larger twigs and sticks.

By the time Calvin came back, a nice little fire was blazing.

"Looked," Calvin said. "No deer."

"My bad," Gus said. "Could have sworn I saw one. Thanks for checking."

The three men cut spit-forks out of relatively straight branches—Calvin using a flint knife that was actually pretty sharp—and hung chunks of venison and grouse to roast over the fire. Hack passed out some raw nuts Hack had gathered from the same health food store where he'd chased down the grouse.

"What, no berries?" Gus asked him.

The three men chowed down. All three tossed occasional chunks to Shakey, who squatted on the edge of the fire's glow and seemed in the end to wind up with a bigger share than any of the others.

Shakey wasn't one to waste time chewing. He just gobbled and gulped and swallowed. Calvin did likewise.

Hack and Gus took a more leisurely approach. Hack savored each bite of his meat and nuts, all of which turned out delicious. By the time winter's early darkness drifted around them, Hack felt stuffed and satisfied. "Paleo's not all bad," he observed.

Gus said, "A shame we got no beer."

"Beer is Neo," Calvin said.

"Wouldn't you just know?" Gus said to Hack.

Gus asked Calvin. "It'll be dark soon and it's going to get a lot colder. Where do you sleep around here?"

"Cave," Calvin said.

"You mean the mineshaft?" Hack asked.

"No," Calvin said. "Cave."

Gus said to Hack, "I brought my sleep gear in my pack. How about you?"

"Of course," Hack said. Then, "Calvin, you want to show us your cave?"

The three men tossed Shakey the last few meat chunks. He dispatched them.

The men dumped snow on the fire to put it out. Calvin led Hack and Gus on a narrow path through the trees. Shakey tagged along. They passed over a small bluff that looked out over open farm fields. On the other side of the fields, Hack spotted lights from a small cluster of houses about a half mile in the distance.

"Do you know who lives there?" Hack asked Calvin.

Calvin looked sad. "Neos," he said.

"Neos?" Gus asked.

But Hack recognized the word. He asked, "As opposed to Paleos?"

Calvin nodded.

Hack asked, "From GC?"

Calvin nodded again.

Hack felt a stirring of excitement. "I'd like to check that out."

Gus said, "Why?"

"For Sam's case," Hack said. "The original reason we came out here."

"Tomorrow," Gus said. "Tonight, we take cover from the cold."

30 Calvin's Cave

"Liberating tolerance, then, would mean intolerance against movements from the Right, and toleration of movements from the Left."

Herbert Marcuse

While Gus stepped off the path to relieve himself, Hack and Shakey followed Calvin for what turned out to be only a twenty-minute stroll along a decent trail.

Up ahead, Hack saw a crevice among some elevated rocks. "It that your cave?"

"Yes," Calvin said.

"Have you used this cave before?"

"No," Calvin said. "New."

When they were about fifteen feet from the crevice, Shakey spotted something on the ground and began to sniff at it. While Calvin went on ahead, Hack stopped to look at Shakey's find for himself. It was a dark curled tube about eight inches long and two inches in diameter, shaped like a bent black boomerang.

Shakey gave a single yip and backed away from the tube. Hack leaned over to inspect it. It looked dry and hard. Its scent was mildly spicy, but pleasant.

Gus came up alongside. Hack pointed down and asked him, "Do you know what this is?"

"Shit," Gus muttered.

"What?"

Gus shook his head and said again. "Shit."

"What do you mean?"

"I just said. It's a fecal plug."

"What's that?"

But Gus ignored him and motored his bulk up to Calvin, who had just reached the front of the cave.

Gus tugged gently on Calvin's fur cloak. Very quietly, he murmured, "Calvin!"

Calvin turned to look at him, curious.

Hack joined the other two. Shakey slunk along, growling a low growl. He glared into the cave with almost bulging eyes. His tremor intensified.

Something or someone was humming high pitched sounds from the darkness inside the cave.

"What's that?" Hack whispered.

The humming turned to squeals and then growling.

Hack took one step closer and peered in and saw the dark rounded form of a curled-up bear. Two tiny black forms nestled against her. Cubs.

The last light of the sun flashed in the mother bear's wide-open glaring eyes. She popped her jaws and huffed and snorted and began to stand, but she was lethargic and groggy and stiff, as anyone would be who had spent most of her past weeks curled up asleep.

"Idiots," Gus whispered, "Don't you recognize a fecal plug? It's what a hibernating bear dumps. If we don't move our own asses right now, she'll mix us into the next turd she squeezes out her ass."

The three men backed down the little elevation. When they reached flat ground, they pointed themselves back where they came from and broke into clumsy sprints. Shakey's white slim body bulleted ahead.

Hack envied Shakey's footspeed but took the lead on the other two men. As the ancient joke said, he only had to beat one of them. After about two hundred yards, he stopped to recover his wind and bent over and put his hands on his knees. Calvin went blazing by. Gus caught up with Hack and stopped and bent over himself, breathing even harder.

Hack gasped out to Gus, "Will she follow us?"

"Probably not," Gus said. "She won't leave her cubs behind. And if we're lucky, she'll think she dreamed us. Like you dream a Thanksgiving dinner with turkey and stuffing and mashed potatoes and cranberries. By now, she should be crashed for the winter again."

"Should be?'

Hack and Gus caught up with Calvin and Shakey back at the site of their earlier fire and meal. Using makeshift brooms they assembled from branches, Hack and Gus cleared the snow out of a fifteen-foot space around their previous fire area. Hack and Gus started a new fire. This time, Gus used his lighter openly and Calvin said nothing. Calvin sat on the ground looking away into the starry darkness, in the direction of the lights of the houses where he'd said the Neos lived.

Gus unrolled a long thick black pelt from his pack and set it on the ground by Calvin.

Hack asked, "Is that a real fur?"

"All organic," Gus said. "Bear, coincidentally enough. My great-great-grandpa killed it."

"I remember that rug." Hack said. "From your rec room."

"So? It's real fur. Satisfies Calvin's rules. Right, Calvin?"

Calvin picked it up and sniffed it and nodded and curled up and swaddled himself in it and lay down. In less than a minute he was snoring. Shakey climbed on top of him and curled and started snoring right along with Calvin.

Hack and Gus each took out their own more modern winter gear, including micro-thin insulated blankets and sleeping bags rated down to 25 below zero Fahrenheit.

Nevertheless, it was cold: "Shakey," Gus whispered. "Get over here."

Shakey kept snoring.

"Dammit," Gus whispered to Hack. "You'd think the mutt would remember who gives him his beer."

"You said it yourself," Hack said, "Dogs love smells."

"I could use the warmth of another body."

"Don't look at me," Hack said. "And don't bother to whisper. They've both crashed for the night."

"It's been years since I slept on winter ground outdoors," Gus said. "I must be getting soft."

"Been only a year for me," Hack said. "Last January I did a bunch of nights in a hollow log."

"Wish you were cozy in that log now, don't you?"

Hack said nothing.

Gus asked, "Have you wondered how long our batshit buddy survived out here this long?"

"I told you, he's not a buddy. He's a witness. For Sam's case."

"Do you know what he's witness to?"

"That's what I'm hoping to find out," Hack said. "Something to do with Rick Kadlec and his bunch. Or maybe the Neos. Sam needs an alternate suspect. A Real Killer."

"Neos?"

Hack gave Gus a summary of what he knew about the *Annals* and the GC factions. Then: "As far as surviving, I suspect Calvin spent most of the recent cold spell in my basement."

"With you and Mattie?"

"No, that's Mattie's basement, remember? In her house," Hack said. "I'm talking about the basement of my own old house. From my Mom and Dad."

"Where they killed Amir? You finally went back?"

"Yeah."

"Rough for you?"

"Not good," Hack said. "And on top of the original nightmare, Calvin made a big mess down there."

Gus said, "You need some help cleaning it out?"

Good to have a friend. "You'd do that? That'd be nice. It's really a mess."

"It is nice, but I was actually thinking more of sending LG over. He's young and limber and he works cheap."

Another bubble popped. "I'll let you know."

Another pause. Hack was almost asleep when Gus said, "You do realize if we leave this witness buddy of yours out on his own in these woods, in one day, or maybe two at the most, he'll be taking the permanent dirt nap?"

"I know that."

"You planning to follow him around out here the rest of your life?"

Hack answered, "You planning to let him starve or freeze to death or wander into another bear den?"

More silence.

Soon Hack heard Gus snoring and soon after that Hack was asleep himself.

31 Gynodelphia

"Gaea is Mother to all. And she needs no man to procreate. Our original Mother Gaea gave birth to the heavens, the mountains and the sea all by herself, without help from any male."

-Gaea Free, *Annals of Internal GC Struggle*

Hack woke up curled in his sleeping bag. He was lying on his left side. When he rolled over onto his back, thousands of tiny needles pricked his left arm. He lay motionless a few moments, waiting for the needles to go away and for his shoulder to loosen enough for him to move his arm.

He felt groggy as a mama bear jolted out of hibernation. He opened his eyes. Gus was still sleeping. The fire was out.

Once the prickling subsided, Hack steeled himself and shuffled out of his sleeping bag into the cold morning air. He grabbed his boots off the nearby ground and pulled them on and laced them up.

He climbed upright and spent the next two minutes hopping about on the dry ground around the campfire.

When Hack stopped, he saw Gus's shaggy bearded head poking out of his bag, watching Hack.

"Trying to warm up," Hack explained.

"Notice anything?" Gus asked.

"Now that you mention," Hack said.

Calvin and Shakey were both gone.

Gus got up and Hack and Gus took turns relieving themselves among the nearby trees. They snacked on breakfast bars and water while they packed up their overnight gear. They put out the fire and took off after Calvin and Shakey.

When they reached the same bluff at which Calvin had paused late yesterday, they saw Calvin's trail of two big footprints and Shakey's trail of four small paw prints leading down the hill and across the fields towards the little cluster of houses. Gus and Hack followed.

About a quarter of a mile from the first house, they saw a wooden sign with neat hand printed letters:

GYNODELPHIA
A Woman's Place
No Men—No Rape Vibes

Hack and Gus glanced at each other and shrugged and kept walking.

About a hundred yards before reaching the first house, Hack heard what was at first registered only as a faint keening sound. As he and Gus got closer, the keening resolved first into shrieking mingled with wailing and then into distinct words, one of which he recognized with a start was the shouted word "Rape!" again and again—"Rape!"

Hack ran towards the awful word. He passed the front of the first house and turned left into a small side yard filled with a dozen or more women. One was confronting Calvin, who—to Hack's relief—stood flatfooted, helpless and dumbfounded.

Off a few yards to the side, three women clustered around another who lay on her back on the ground.

As he pushed through the crowd, Hack flashed on the odd fact that all the women seemed to be wearing identical woven pink hats rounded on top like domes, pulled down over their ears, trailing pairs of pink braided tassels, one on each side.

Hack reached ground zero of the tumult: Shakey had mounted a smaller yellow-brown Yorkshire Terrier from behind and was working with his characteristic drive and enthusiasm.

In the same instant, Hack realized it was his old GC nemesis Tiff Madden herself who was standing in front of Calvin and screaming at him. Her mouth frothed in rage—Hack saw actual bubbles around her lips.

Calvin stood in a crouching posture, his shoulders bent in the eternal male shrug, signifying What did I do? What can I do? Why look at me?

"You brought him!" Tiff shrieked. "You brought this beast to—to *rape*—our Artemis!"

Calvin gestured at Artemis with both hands out front, as if he were shoveling Tiffs attention towards the dogs. "Consent?"

Tiff poked his chest with a stiff index finger. "When? When did she consent?"

Hack checked the dogs for himself. Artemis didn't look non-consenting, but with dogs it was hard to tell. At least she wasn't trying to get away. But how could she, with Shakey mounted on her and impaling her from behind?

Shakey did his work with short rapid repeated thrusts. Artemis returned her own back-and-forth movements in sync with Shakey. Hack supposed her cooperation might count at least as a nonverbal expression of consent.

Artemis's facial expression was unreadable. But then, he didn't know her personally.

Gus huffed up behind Hack and stopped. He took a look at the scene and said, "You got to be kidding."

Tiff turned on him. "Who the hell are you?"

"Shakey's owner," Gus said.

She advanced towards Gus. "Shakey? Is that supposed to be funny? You think rape is funny?"

Hack stepped between them. "Shakey's the dog's name, that's all. Because of his idiopathic tremor."

She glanced at the two dogs and narrowed her eyes. "What tremor? I don't see any tremor." Hack followed her glance. She was right. Shakey's head held steady as a rock. For now, no tremor.

She swung her anger on Hack. "You! Wilder! I should have known you'd be involved in this."

"There is no 'this'," he said. "It's just dogs doing dogs."

At that moment, Shakey and Artemis finished the first stage of their coitus. Now Shakey swung his leg over Artemis's back and stood behind her so that they stood butt-to-butt facing away from each other.

Tiff bent down to grab Shakey. Gus barked, "Don't!"

She glanced up. Gus said, "It's a dog knot. She's locked him into herself. If you pull them apart, you can hurt them both."

She said, "How long will this atrocity go on?"

Gus said, "Maybe five minutes. Maybe forty-five. If you want to do something helpful, get down there with her and pet your dog or something."

Tiff advanced on Gus and poked his huge chest with her index finger. She said, "Our Artemis has to endure this torture another forty-five minutes?"

Gus said, "Lady, do you actually know anything about dogs?"

She hissed, "My name is Gaea Free."

"Whatever," Gus said. "Well, Miss or Mrs. Gaea Free, dogs don't decide on sex like humans do."

"I don't need some macho hypertrophied male lecturing me about being female," she said. "I live that experience. Every day."

Gus said, "Can't you tell this bitch is in heat? Have you lived that experience too?"

Her face purpled with yet more rage.

Gus paid no never-mind. "With dogs, females decide. Male dogs have sex with female dogs because females trigger them. Your Artemis here was shooting out hormones in every direction, to every canine in smelling distance"—Gus waved his thick arms all about—"announcing she was ready for action. Shakey had no choice but to follow his nose and his dick. Any lack of consent was all on Shakey's side."

"You're blaming Artemis? The victim?"

"I'll bet she did something to get him going, didn't she?"

"What? Wear a short skirt?"

"Did she present her rear? Back up towards him? Lift her tail and flick it in his face?"

The three other women had helped the fallen woman up. She brushed the snow off her coat and walked over and stood next to Tiff. If anything, she looked even more enraged. Her eyes shone with a wild light.

"I'm Thalassa Free," she announced, as if that explained something. She was a short round woman with curly black hair. She placed her hands on her hips and glared at Gus, her eyes bulging in mania. She pulled a short flint knife with a bone handle from the belt of her big skirt under her white robe and began waving it in trembling circles. The women who had been helping her gathered by her. All the women surrounded the three men.

The women began keening and shrieking, howling, rolling their eyes, tearing at their robes. Thalassa Free raised one arm and they all stopped in an instant. In a low voice, she began chanting "Rape!" and the other women joined in, intoning: "Rape! Rape! Rape!"

To Hack, it was unnerving. Gus towered over everyone, but more than a dozen women surrounded them. And one was swinging a deadly weapon in the air in front of her.

Tiff raised her own arm and in in an instant the chanting stopped.

"You males better get out of here," Tiff hissed into the sudden eerie quiet. "You've got no right to be in Gynodelphia in the first place. This is a male-free zone."

Gus shook his head. "I'm not leaving without Shakey."

Thalassa waved her knife in bigger circles.

Calvin shouted "Finished!" and pointed to the dogs.

Shakey and Artemis had chosen that moment to separate. Artemis wandered towards the back yard. In his own cavalier way, Shakey strolled about five yards over to a dry grassless spot of dirt next to the house. He rotated three times doggy style and curled up and laid his head down on his feet and closed his eyes.

Calvin was already on his way, heading along the side of the house towards the front. He turned and called back over his shoulder, "Shakey."

Shakey opened his eyes and saw Calvin and got up and followed him.

Hack said to Gus, "Let's go."

Gus shot one last glare at Gaea Free and turned and followed Shakey. Just in case, Hack shepherded Gus from behind.

The women began chanting again, "Rape! Rape! Rape!"

After about thirty feet, the four males reached the front of the house. Gus turned and shouted back at the women, "If there's puppies, I get half!"

Tiff stood with her hands on her hips. "Women run things here!" She yelled. "There won't be any puppies!"

"Go!" Calvin said, "Now!" He began jogging towards the bluff. Shakey gamboled past him, leading the way with even more verve and energy than usual, as if he were in an unusually sporty mood.

Gus and Hack trudged across the field after the two pace setters.

As they passed the sign, Hack stopped and glanced back at Gynodelphia. It seemed like the kind of place Tiff Madden would manage. The house was rickety and dilapidated. Assorted tools leaned helter-skelter against the sides of the buildings, whose cracked sidings desperately needed paint. Hack wondered how long the peaked red-shingled roofs could hold up under the mass of high-piled snow.

The women—the Neos, of course—had worn shaggy brown cloaks that might have been rawhide. Some kept smatterings of fur. They were pinned together with bone fasteners. He wondered where the women got the hides and bones if they didn't hunt. A few wore necklaces of striped yellow and brown zebra shell mussels, the invasive species lately crowding northland waterways.

Shakey and Calvin zipped up the little bluff and turned and waited. When Hack and Gus joined them at the top of the bluff, Gus stopped and glared across the fields back towards Gynodelphia. He said, "People who don't understand dogs shouldn't have dogs."

"True enough," Hack said.

Gus waved his right hand at Calvin. Gus said, "And people who don't know the outdoors shouldn't live outdoors."

"Also true."

"With luck their ignorance will give those women what they got coming. But what about Calvin?"

"I've been working that out," Hack said. Then he said, "Calvin!"

Calvin looked at Hack.

"Calvin," Hack told him. "Whatever happens, stick with me. Got it?"

Calvin nodded.

Gus asked Hack, "You got a plan?"

"I'm taking him home," Hack said.

32 Gaea Free

"What is moral is what helps the Struggle. The Struggle needs the Movement. Therefore, what helps the Movement is moral; what hurts the Movement is immoral."

Gaea Free, *Annals of Internal GC Struggle*

It was obvious. Of course, Gaea Free was Tiff Madden. Hack should have seen it coming. Who else?

The only apparent change in Tiff from Hack's GC days was her plain brown hair. At GC her hair had changed color week to week, sometimes even from day to day, from blue to orange and to pink and back to blue again, then platinum white, then flaming scarlet. And so on. Brown must be its original shade.

Hack's theory was that people who continually change their names or their hair color or their tattoos lack some essential sense of identity. Since they don't know who they are from the inside, they're always trying on new outsides.

But he wasn't sure his theory accounted for Tiff. Even under the name Gaea, she was still the essential Tiff. She still sported the same contemptuous expression she'd always worn and cocked her head back in the same smug arrogant way, like she was just waiting for you to do or say or think some vile thing so she could pounce in disgust.

His own reactive disgust gave him a shock. He had to admit he hated the woman. It wasn't healthy for a man to hate like that, and the power of his emotion clashed with his self-image as well-intentioned human being, but it was true. Even years later, the sight and sound of her still incited rage in his gut.

As they hiked through the woods towards Gus's house, Shakey ranged off their trail far and wide. Calvin now hung back about twenty feet behind Hack and Gus, following Hack as commanded.

Hack said to Gus, "Don't experts say you should wait until a dog's something like a year old before breeding him?"

"That's one opinion. Artemis disagrees."

"Obviously."

"And Shakey goes along with her. He's like that."

A hundred yards later, Gus asked, "What were those things they wore on their heads? Little knitted pink domes with tassels?—like something out of the old *Star Trek*, the original TV show with the cheap costumes and crappy special effects."

"You mean the hats."

"Were those vagina hats?" Gus asked. "Like in the news? I never saw one in real life."

"No, those were uterus hats. The two hanging tassels were meant to represent ovarian tubes."

"What happened to the vagina hats?"

"Not woke enough."

"What does that mean?"

Hack said, "Gaea Free—the woman you just met, the one I knew as Tiff Madden back at GC—she wrote about it in the *Annals*. The vagina hat isn't a sufficiently powerful symbol. It's a mere frontal representation of the apparatus. They wanted something that goes deeper. So, uterus hats."

"You mean, deeper physically?"

"I don't mean anything. But Gaea Free wants women to express something deeper part of the female essence. To embrace their true inner nature."

"Which is?"

"Our modern word hysteria comes from the Greek word for uterus. In her theory of feminism, the uterus hat stands for hysteria. She says the Greeks slandered all things female as part of their patriarchal oppression. As part of putting women down. the Greeks made out like hysteria is a bad thing, when it is really a good thing because—her idea, not mine—hysteria is an authentic female thing, like a uterus is an authentic female thing. She advises women to get in touch with their inner hysteric. She thinks wearing a uterus hat will help with that."

"Because hysteria is female?"

"That's what she wrote," Hack said.

"That's quite a theory," Gus said. "Almost impossible to believe."

"Almost," Hack agreed. "But hysteria isn't just a theory. It's a serious psychological condition in the real world. People who suffer from hysteria lose control over their thoughts and emotions. I've read it afflicts millions of people. And ninety percent are women."

"Yep." Gus gave a sage nod. "And the other ten are gay men."

There was no topper for that. Hack stopped and waited for Calvin. Gus waited along with Hack. When Calvin came shambling along, Hack asked him, "Calvin, do you know what Gaea Free and those women are even doing in that place?"

Calvin stopped and looked at Hack like it was obvious. "Neos farm," he said. "Not hunt."

"I didn't see any sign of any farming," Hack said.

"Not yet," Calvin said. "Spring."

Gus seemed to get Calvin's point. Gus asked, "So these Neo women just moved in recently, right?"

Calvin nodded.

"And they claim they're going to begin farming once spring comes?" Gus asked.

Calvin nodded again.

Gus said, "Do they know as much about farming as they do about dogs?"

Calvin's lips quivered in what was almost a smile—to Hack, a welcome sign of a remnant humanity hiding underneath. Maybe the old Calvin still lurked in there somewhere, buried under the dirt and hair, behind the broken front tooth.

"What I don't get," Hack asked Calvin, "Is why did you trespass onto their land? You must know they don't want any males around."

Calvin looked mournful. "Tiff," he said. "Love."

"God help us," Gus said.

33 Explaining To Mattie

"It's tough to stay married. My wife kisses the dog on the lips, yet she won't drink from my glass."

Rodney Dangerfield

The next afternoon, Mattie asked Hack, "Who'll feed him?"

"Me," Hack said. "Please?"

They stood next to each other in the kitchen looking out through the window into the back yard. Calvin and Shakey were snuggling together in the new paleo-qualified shelter Gus and Hack had built them out of branches and leaves.

Mattie said, "Promise?"

"Promise. Please? I really want to keep him."

"And you'll clean up after him?"

"I'll do that too. Please, I really want to keep him."

"I don't know," she said. "I just know I'll be the one who winds up cleaning all his big messes."

"The messes won't be so big."

"You do know I'm talking about Calvin, don't you?"

"Of course," Hack said, "I'm hoping in the end Shakey will head back to his real home at Gus's."

She said, "I don't know about that either. Shakey seems pretty attached to Calvin."

In his little hut, Calvin wrapped Gus's bearskin rug more tightly over himself and Shakey leaned up against him and closed his eyes. In an instant they were both asleep.

"Did you see how ticked off Gus was?" Mattie asked, "When Shakey refused to hop in his truck to go home with him?"

"He'll get over it. Gus believes in personal freedom."

"What about LG? Shakey is LG's dog, right? What happens when LG comes back home?"

"It'll all sort itself out."

"Like everything else, right?" Mattie asked. She turned away from the window and walked out of the kitchen into the living room. Hack followed her.

She plopped down onto the couch and sighed.

He sat on the couch to her right. Her first impulse seemed to be to lean away, but then she put her right hand on his left arm and leaned her head on his shoulder.

He asked, "Is something the matter? I mean, lately?"

"Long story," she said.

"You can tell me," he said, "Anytime you want."

"I know," she said. "Just not now."

He felt her begin to cry, little shudders soft against his shoulder. Hack said nothing. What was there to say?

34 Feds

"(a) …whoever, in any matter within the jurisdiction of the executive, legislative, or judicial branch of the Government of the United States, knowingly and willfully

(1) falsifies, conceals, or covers up by any trick, scheme, or device a material fact;

(2) makes any materially false, fictitious, or fraudulent statement or representation; or

(3) makes or uses any false writing or document knowing the same to contain any materially false, fictitious, or fraudulent statement or entry;

shall be…imprisoned not more than 5 years…"

18 U.S. Code § 1001

It was the middle of the day, but after a few minutes Mattie complained to Hack that she was tired and got up from the couch and went into the bedroom to nap.

Why was Mattie so listless lately? Normally Mattie was a dynamo. A fireball. Mattie was a creature of brash impulse, a woman who ripped doors almost off their hinges and busted drawers open and slammed them closed. She sliced onions like a serial killer, slamming the knife with thunderous thwacks down on the cutting board.

Mattie had once cut most of his ear clean off a terrorist. Hack had seen Mattie slam a garbage can lid into the head of a barroom troublemaker, then joke about it the next moment.

But now? She seemed lethargic. Slow moving. Melancholy.

She had even gained a little weight—but mostly in erogenous zones, he reminded himself, and smiled at the cliché. He mentally face-slapped himself. Get off that. How could he help her? That's what mattered.

The doorbell rang.

Which was strange right from the get-go. No one rang that bell. Their few friends like Gus and LG just rambled right in. And Hack hadn't ordered a pizza.

Hack stood and went to the door and opened it.

Two men stood on the little concrete stoop, both dressed in identical camel hair dress coats, open enough at the top to display the collars of dark suits and white shirts and neckties.

Uh oh.

One looked to be in his forties. His gray hair was cut very short. He wore big black framed glasses. A wiry muscular neck emerged from his tight white collar. He looked grim, angry, and determined. John Lennon had this guy in mind when he wrote about that "all-American bullet-headed Saxon mother's son."

The other was on the taller side, thinner and older, with whitening hair and thick black brows and a mournful look seemingly stitched into his hound dog face.

The younger one said, "Mr. Wilder? Nathanael Wilder?"

Hack said nothing.

The younger one said, "Mr. Wilder, if that's who you are, I'm Agent MacNutt and this is Agent Blanding. May we come in?"

They both flashed little leather cases with federal-looking ID's in them.

In response, Hack stepped out onto the little concrete slab in front and closed the door behind him. He leaned back against the house and folded his arms against the cold and waited.

"You are Nathanael Wilder?" Agent MacNutt asked again.

Hack said nothing. He focused on mastering the twitch in his belly and keeping his face expressionless.

Blanding said, "We have some questions we'd like to ask you."

Hack said nothing.

MacNutt asked, "Is there some reason you're not responding verbally?"

"Is there some specific reason you're not letting us in?" Blanding asked.

The two agents looked at each other: Blanding raised his thick black eyebrows. MacNutt shrugged back.

"This is ridiculous," MacNutt said to Hack. "Of course, you don't have to speak—at this moment—though eventually we can require you to talk with us. In the meantime, there's nothing stopping us from speaking to you."

Hack stuck with his poker face.

"Let's start at the beginning," Blanding said. "With Penn Lajoie's murder."

"Assuming that is the beginning," MacNutt said. He looked around with open disgust at the shabby slat-sided houses and wide snow-covered yards of Ojibwa City. Hack promptly despised him. Hack knew theirs was a poor town. He also knew he loved it.

Shakey bolted into the front yard from the side of the house. He rocked to a sudden stop in the snow about thirty feet away. He locked into a fighting stance, his young but already powerful chest thrust forward. He glared at the two agents, trembling. Or was that just his tremor? If so, it seemed worse than usual.

Blanding said, "Is that a wolf?"

MacNutt said, "It's white, Jim."

"There are white wolves," Blanding said.

"Not very many," MacNutt said. He unbuttoned his overcoat, letting it fall open in front.

Hack took that as a threat to Shakey. He was about to give up his silence and say something when Calvin dashed around the corner, clad in his long fur cloak and fur boots, carrying his spear.

Shakey trembled harder and lifted his head and bared his teeth and began howling a high-pitched howl that soared up and down in register and pitch. Calvin opened his mouth and began to screech like Shakey. He danced back and forth from one foot to the other on his scrawny naked legs. He lifted his spear above his head with both hands. Shakey glanced up at Calvin and copied his dance, rocking sideways on his own four legs.

MacNutt and Blanding exchanged glances. MacNutt shook his head and said something to Hack, but the canine whining and human howling drowned out his words. Blanding put both black-gloved hands over his ears.

MacNutt spoke again. Hack opened his hands in front of him and painted an apologetic "Sorry, can't hear you" look on his face.

Then Hack blurted out, "Huskies can't bark, only howl," and instantly regretted it, wondering in that instant if even making simple factual statement might open him to prosecution for lying— what if the feds showed up in court with a husky that could bark?

Didn't matter. The two agents couldn't hear him anyway. MacNutt glared at Hack. Blanding glared too. He and MacNutt shook their heads and exchanged more glances and retreated to the car they had parked in front of the house. They got in. MacNutt rolled down his passenger window and shouted something Hack couldn't hear. From Hack's limited lipreading skill, it might have been "Catch you later!" They drove away.

Hack turned to the two howlers. "Quiet!" he roared.

Calvin and Shakey silenced and bent their heads and looked down towards the ground in gestures of canine submission.

Mattie opened the door and stepped out. She ignored Calvin and Shakey and asked Hack, "What in the hell is going on out here?"

Calvin and Shakey slunk back into the side yard again and disappeared, leaving Hack to face her disapproval alone.

Mattie demanded again, "Well?"

"Feds," he said. "Or so they claimed. Calvin and Shakey drove them off with that racket."

"Feds? That's all we need." She paused. "Sam's fault, I bet. Come in. You'll freeze."

He came in. Mattie turned her back on him and stalked back into her bedroom and slammed the door behind her. Which was more like the Mattie he knew, so this was good, right?

He grabbed a Chumpster from the fridge and went down to the basement couch to suck it down.

The more Hack thought, the more ticked off he got. Who did these feds think they were? Wasn't Blanding one of the same FBI pricks who tried to railroad him last year? That's right. It was Blanding who slandered Hack all over ZNN and the other media as a "person of interest" in his friend Amir's murder and warned Hack to turn himself in. And hadn't Blanding been one of the FBI agents whose "lack of candor" ticked off the Judge so much he canceled any prosecution completely? For prosecutorial misconduct?

The more Hack thought, the gladder he was that he had listened to Sam. Sam had advised him a few years ago never to talk anyone from the U.S. government.

At the time, it seemed paranoid. They were sharing lunchtime Chumpsters and pizza in a booth in Lazzeri's, a fancy Italian place on St. Peter Street in downtown St. Paul. Hack didn't recall how the subject came up, but Sam warned him. "Never talk to any fed ever."

Hack asked, "You mean, like FBI agents?"

Sam stabbed the air with the same skinny index finger he deployed to spear lying witnesses. "Not just the FBI. Don't talk to any fed any time. You name it—Department of Justice, Department of Agriculture, U.S. Board on Geographic Names, doesn't matter."

"U.S. Board on Geographic Names? Who's that?"

"They decide official names for geographic features, like rivers and mountains and glaciers and the like."

"And I can't suggest a name to them? Why not?"

"Because of the perjury trap."

Sam ignored the frosty mug the waiter had set on their table and took a swig straight from his Chumpster bottle. "You see, under our current totalitarian semi-fascist federal law, lying to any federal official at any time, or even concealing information on any matter within federal government jurisdiction—which the feds consider pretty much everything inside America or out of it—is a crime. Even denying your guilt of a crime is itself a crime."

"I didn't know that," Hack said.

Sam was just warming up. "When feds want to convict somebody of something, which is always, and they need testimony, which is always, they need witnesses, right?"

Sam slammed his own Chumpster back on the table so hard the white foam frothed over the lip of the bottle and slid down its neck. "Whatever you say about anything can get you in trouble, like what you knew or didn't know, or when something happened, or misremembering two events as happening in the wrong order.

"Take the way you remember a conversation," Sam said. "All they have to do is find some other witness who remembers the conversation differently. They can choose to believe him over you and now you've lied to the feds. Then they got you. They can use the threat of prison to extort any testimony they want from you to use against someone else. Lather, rinse, repeat."

"But you get your chance at trial."

"They might not convict you, but even if you're ultimately acquitted, the trial itself is a punishment. And they're playing with taxpayer money. If it threatens to run out, they just print more. Can you do that?"

"All federal prosecutors can't be like that," Hack said.

"They don't all have to be. For you, it's a risk-reward calculation. Even if the risk of running into a bent prosecutor is small, the price you pay is huge."

Hack said, "This seems kind of paranoid, even to me, and I'm known for my paranoia. I wonder if you're not just talking like a frustrated defense lawyer, who always thinks his clients are innocent, or at least pretends to. Or maybe you're just mad about some bad trial outcome you just had."

"What are you talking about?"

"Well, what about you?" Hack asked. "You say stuff to the feds all the time."

"Me? I'm an Officer of the Court. I don't talk in the role of a witness. You, on the other hand, any time they get a peep out of you, you're a witness. And they don't see you as a person. To them you're just so much roadkill. You're nothing but a skunk in the middle of the road, one they're eager to flatten in their chase after someone else, even if your sad stink trails them for a few miles afterwards and gives them a few moments of conscience. Assuming they have any."

Hack said, "It can't be bad as you say. People do commit real crimes. And the feds do convict them.

"Almost always, actually. Ninety-seven percent of the time, I think."

"They must have real evidence."

"So?"

"So how can the government put criminals in jail if witnesses don't cooperate?"

"How is that your problem?"

"Because I don't want crooks wandering around committing more crimes," Hack said.

"You don't?" Sam's eyes had shrunk to slits. "Why not?"

"Maybe I'm a good citizen."

"Maybe." Sam bared his teeth in his thin shark smile. "I suppose I concede for the sake of argument you are a good citizen, in a limited hangout half-assed sort of a way. But I can imagine circumstances where the feds won't think so. And they might think it worthwhile to nail you or use you to nail someone else, maybe even by having you testify to some lies they pretend to believe."

"Doesn't that make them liars?"

"Who's going to punish them for that? You know, they can lie to you any time they want, right?"

Hack did know that much. Cops could lie to suspects and witnesses. And did.

Sam said, "And like any behavior that rewards a person with money and promotions and status and more money, lying can become a profitable habit. Maybe even an addiction."

Hack sipped his own beer and pondered. Then, "So, if the feds ever come talk to me, what do I do?"

"Nothing. You do nothing. You say nothing."

"Just refuse to answer?"

"No, refusing to answer is saying something. I mean literally nothing."

"I'll feel like a fool."

"You'll get over it. Just imagine how brilliant you'd feel sitting in a cell."

"If they ask questions, I just glue my lips together and stare?"

Sam employed his one-slow-word-at-a-time-because-I'm-talking-to-an-idiot voice. "Are you even listening? Exactly. If you don't speak, you can't lie. You can't even be accused of lying. Nothing."

"I just stare back like an idiot."
"Yes. Type casting. After a while, they'll get bored and leave."
"Then what?"
"Then you call me."

35 *A Suicide in St. Paul*

Hack did call Sam, who said "The Feds did what? They came to you without going through me?"

"Yes."

"Did you tell them you're working for me on a case?"

"No, I said nothing. Like you said."

"Literally?"

"Literally. I just stared back at them like a statue."

"Well, at least that's something," Sam said. "But they shouldn't be talking to anyone who works for me. But maybe they don't even know about that. Seems unlikely, though. I'll take it up with Judge Carlson, although come to think of it, he's a state court judge and these were the feds. Maybe I need to yell at someone else."

"Please do."

"Meanwhile, have you found anything at all that helps Rick?"

"Not really," Hack said. "Did you read the entire memo?"

"Yes. I agree that there's no help for Rick in the *Annals*, at least so far. But keep digging. I need a Real Killer."

"I will."

Sam hung up.

Hack went back into the kitchen. He checked on Calvin and Shakey in the back yard and confirmed they had cuddled up together back in their hut.

He sat down at his computer and learned in the most mundane possible way what had happened to the GC Meso Mel Untermeyer: he read it on the local paper's website, in an archived article from three months previous:

Local Man Dead In Apparent Suicide

Ojibwa City *Savage*
Dateline: St. Paul

By Staff Writer Norton Shandling

Mel Untermeyer, an Ojibwa College of Minnesota graduate and former Ojibwa City resident, was found dead in his yard in St. Paul Thursday morning. Authorities say he hanged himself from a backyard oak with a hand-braided hemp rope.

Mr. Untermeyer had moved from San Francisco to St. Paul to work for software giant Gogol Checkov. His coworker Victor Radke told the *Savage*: "Mel was a hard worker and a good guy. He didn't deserve what happened to him. But he was very sensitive, too sensitive for this world. I sometimes even wondered if he had Asperger's. Couldn't handle the cut and thrust of debate."

Given the ongoing prosecution of Gogol Checkov coworker Rick Kadlec for an alleged politically motived bombing, it was natural for this reporter to ask Mr. Radke whether the "cut and thrust" to which he referred had to do with some contention within Gogol Checkov.

Mr. Radke declined to answer specifically. He did say, "The accusations really hurt him. Especially coming from someone he trusted. I think it humiliated him. I know it broke his heart."

It has been confirmed that some months ago, Gogol Checkov fired Mr. Untermeyer after female coworkers accused him of sexual abuse.

At the time, GC posted a written statement on its website: "This week, allegations of abuse have come to light regarding Mel Untermeyer, who worked for us as developer on our industry leading search engine PrivaNation. We take such complaints seriously as a collective. As a result, and after some agonizing consideration, we are letting Mel go."

Mr. Untermeyer was apparently despondent over several failed romantic relationships and over being unable to find any new work in his field.

Hack realized who the "Mel" in the GC Annals was. And why he had disappeared from the Annals six months previous. GC had fired him—in something like the same way they had fired Hack years before.

But how did this new guy Victor Radke fit in?

36 Future Sapiens Strikes Again

"We will construct a society in which the goal of any intelligent person will be to live entirely unnoticed."

Future Sapiens, *The Annals of Internal GC Struggle*

As Sam had asked, Hack went hunting through the *Annals* for more Future Sapiens posts. Hack found this:

Towards An American Social Credit System
From *The Annals of Internal GC Struggle, by Future Sapiens*

China is setting a positive example and a high standard for the U.S. with its new Social Credit System, an admirable tool for improving human behavior.

China employs its more than 600 million surveillance cameras and a myriad other means to monitor both citizens and visitors. China's Social Credit System relies on the monitoring to assign each person a score based on observed activity. Socially undesirable actions range from relatively minor offenses like jaywalking and illegal parking up to serious crimes like robbery and murder.

Of course, expression of ideas inimical to social justice play an important role in calculation of one's score. That is why China monitors and controls all Internet use.

One of the express goals of the System is to disincentivize bad behavior by impoverishing people with low scores. Therefore, one's score determines one's access to schools, employment, travel, bank loans, purchase of property, and all other social and economic opportunities and benefits.

To support its Social Credit System, China is also implementing an "Integrated Joint Operations Platform," which aggregates data from various sources such as cameras, identification checks, and "wifi sniffers." The system captures and subtracts points for even hard-to-spot offenses like inappropriate language.

China's system can be a model for a U.S. Social Credit System ("SCS") of our own. For example, our proposed SCS will assign every person a numerical rating from 100-1000. Simple insertion of one's identity card into a device like an ATM machine could make one's current score immediately available. As in China, the score could be used by all socially, politically and economically significant institutions like banks, stores, universities, and·of course employers.

Our own Gogol Checkov is ideally equipped to design, implement, and maintain the proposed American SCS. As we know, GC already possesses access to every user's Internet history, travel, viewing and reading habits. Implementation of a U.S. version of the Joint Operating Platform would only be an extension of our existing, already robust capacities.

We will also enhance and improve upon China's model. For example, we are looking to development of an artificial intelligence capacity to predict undesirable behavior.

Biotechnology may provide one tool. Hospitals routinely monitor their patients for pulse, blood pressure, breathing and other symptoms. It is likely that very soon portable monitors may become available. We may all be wearing them or may even be required to wear them as a condition of health insurance. As we learn more about mind-body interaction, these portable monitors could become portable "lie detectors" useful in reading wearers' emotional reactions to authority and other stimuli. Eventually the technology may advance to the point of reading wearers' opinions, thereby detecting potential antisocial behavior ahead of time.

Who will control our U.S. Social Credit System? Of course, we can entrust no single individual with this power. We need to create an entity governed by a broad array of stakeholders, including representatives from universities, private corporations, and government, as well as employee and consumer organizations.

Of course, this new entity cannot be subject to the vagaries of politics. The Consumer Financial Protection Board can serve as a model; it was without doubt a step in the right direction.

Of course, an elected President cannot be allowed to interfere. Therefore the SCS must operate independently of the Executive Branch.

SCS funding must be independent of congress; therefore it will draw funding as needed directly from the Federal Reserve.

Most important, the existing Board must select its own members and replacements, preventing outside interference in developing and maintaining consistent policies and practices.

We can address any claims of alleged unconstitutionality by assuring that the U.S. Supreme Court is composed of Justices with a correct understanding of social requirements.

37 VOR

From *The Annals of Internal GC Struggle*, by VOR

I am typing this stream-of-consciousness. I won't stop to edit. When I finish, I'll just post it and see what happens. I'm tired of looking back. I'm tired of looking ahead.

You ask, why? Because of you. You people. You wear me out. You don't want what I offer, which are facts and reason. All you know is your own feelings. Like nobody but you ever had any.

And if I'm going to save even one of you from the maelstrom you're all drowning in, I'll have to join you, I'll have to hurl myself into it myself, boatless, no air tanks, not even fins or water wings.

You ask, why then do I bother to troll you? Why am I here in this Consciousness Team at all? I answer, to warn you: Stop the stupid. Especially stop the stupid ideas. Even good ideas in the end have no reality. All ideas are fig newtons of the imagination (see? I can be whimsical), phantasmagoria, airy nothings, delusions, traps for the unwary and wary alike.

But ideas do have consequences. Stupid ideas have stupid consequences. That's what's sad. You sniff out an idea and then you track it like a bloodhound trailing an escaped convict through the swamp without knowing where it will lead. You never look up or to the left or the right.

You ask me, how can we live without ideas? I don't know. I must be wrong.

I do know you haven't thought your ideas through ahead of time. When you do finally get wherever you're going, some of you will realize you have walked out of the swamp directly off a cliff.

Confused language? Yes. Mixed metaphor? So what? I've decided not to care. Why worry about whether my writing is good or bad? You can't tell the difference anyway.

Some of you already wandered over that cliff. You're like Wile E. Coyote, hanging in the air, destined to plummet to self-destruction the instant you recognize your situation.

Is that a cliché? Sure, but what will you comprehend if not some hackneyed pop culture cliché?

I doubt you've spotted my rotten turns of phrase anyway. Mixing incompatible ideas is an integral aspect of your own derangement. Another cliché: oil and water don't mix. But the oil will still flame up as it sits atop the water. What does that signify? Not sure. But I'll leave it in. No rewrites, that's what I said.

You ask what am I doing on this Consciousness Team when I don't agree with your ideas and when I'm even suspicious of the idea of having ideas at all? I don't know.

Now I remember. To warn you. Maybe one of you will listen and understand. That's my morality. It comes from outside me. That's why I risk all. Despite your threats, I risk all. To save just one of you.

You ask, who tells me to? I answer, God tells me to. Moral principles do exist outside the volatile merely subjective parameters you readjust every week, from day to day, from moment to moment.

You think the idea of God is funny and that I'm crazy to mention such an Entity. You think I am crazy and stupid and evil. But when commanded by another mere human being, you bark like seals and flap your fins in chorus. Some mere human commands "Ork!" and you ask, "How loud?"

At first, I was just curious, like a man who sees a bright neon sign outside a bar promising good times and walks in. Maybe inside he'll find fun, good beer or good live music. He goes through the door and sees a brawl going on and even if it isn't fun at least it's interesting, so he stays to watch. But bottles fly all over the place and skulls crack open and blood spills onto the floor. No fun at all.

You ask, what is wrong with one basing one's thoughts, words and deeds on one's own personal morality? I answer, for one thing, once you do that, the next step is to conclude that anyone who disagrees with you must be basing their words on their own immorality. They must be evil. That is your logic. See where it leads? Murder.

You ask, why do you exaggerate? There's no murder. We oppose all violence. These are just ideas. I ask back, but from where do you obtain your morality in the first place? What do you base it on? You don't know. You decide based on what seems obvious to you at the moment. But where does the obviousness come from?

I ask, how do you know slavery is wrong? Is that obvious? Or genocide? Or racism, sexism, or any other ism? How do you know? Do you know how you know? I know how I know: God created every single human being in the image of God. What do you know?

Those evils could not have been the norm throughout history if their evil were as obvious as you believe.

I say, trust me on this, but you don't even trust yourselves. That's why you wait for others to signal your next crappy theory to you, others who know no more than you nor me nor any mere human being, who are themselves just making it all up as they go.

You ever wonder why they do that? Your leaders? What's in it for them? You think they're not getting something out of you? Out of this? You think?

And you. Without any real God of your own, these other humans become your gods, and you don't even realize it. Or you imagine you yourselves to be gods. Hard to say which is worse.

Whatever you think you know to be moral must be moral, but you don't know how you know, so you wait for someone else to tell you. I ask, how do they know? You don't know how they know any better than you know how you know what you know.

If all that seems confusing, it's because it is an accurate expression of the confused state of your ideas and the lack-logic you employ to derive them, if the word "derived" can honestly be used.

I say, you are repeating an experiment already performed again and again. Check out Auschwitz, Stalin's Terror, the Gulags, the Killing Fields, Rwanda, the Chinese Great Leap Forward and the

Great Cultural Revolution—and those are all from just one century, the century in which for the first time large numbers of people not coincidentally stopped believing in God—horrific events all demonstrating the consequences of the idea that human beings can conjure some morality of their own out of thin air.

You're passing directly from the nineteenth century to the twenty first without learning a thing from the twentieth.

But this time it will be different, you imagine. Because you imagine yourselves to be different. I know you don't trust me, but trust me, you're no better than your forerunners. All you're saying is the product of your solipsism and narcissism and proud ignorance, all mixed together in the same toxic blend that gave us the twentieth century horrors you're headed towards repeating.

I could go on, but why bother? Historically human beings who think morality comes from within themselves have committed the greatest immoralities.

You sense this just enough to scare you away from history and to motivate you to learn as little history as possible. That way you won't have to think about it. But it's one thing to be ignorant, it's another to wave your ignorance as a proud banner as you charge off your cliff and take the rest of us with you.

Your entire lives, you have had the luxury of getting away with your narcissism because the disciplined work was already done before you got here, by people who believed in God and God's morality and worked diligently and intelligently to build an ever richer and more successful world you want to tear down for no intelligible reason you can identify.

The closest you can come is to cite a morality you cannot explain except that it arises from your feelings, which you make a point of refusing to explain, hiding even from yourselves the fact that the real reason you don't explain your feelings is that you can't.

You talk about "lived experience" but you possess almost none, having gone from nursery to suburban enclave to GC bubble without ever needing to live any genuine experience at all.

You think you have awakened to some new kind of true consciousness. Believe me, there's nothing new about you or you so-called consciousness.

And nothing old either. Because you live in an eternal present. This is why in ordinary conversation you cannot construct an intelligible sequence or logical progression of ideas, only one idea at a time in a randomly generated babble to be heard in every college dorm or quad or GC cubicle: "and he's all, and I'm like, and he goes…", one visual after another without causal connection or plot, as if you live a life without theme or purpose—which you do.

I'm getting tiresome.

Reminds me of a story my grandmother told me when I was little:

The Prince and the Pea

Once there was a Prince. And a pea.

The Prince rested on seventy-two layers of cushions and eider down and swaddling. The pea was at the bottom of the pile.

All day everyday hundreds of servants attended on the Prince and gave him whatever he wanted to eat and to drink and to play with. Any game he played he won every time.

Whatever he did was wonderful. All the attendants told the Prince as often as they could spit out the words how they wondered at how wonderful he was to do so many wonderful things so wonderfully.

One day, in the middle of lauding him, one of his attendants mentioned to the Prince how tough and strong and brave the Prince was to survive so much hardship, what with that awful pea down there and all.

The Prince hadn't known about the pea. Truth be told, he couldn't even feel the little nub through all the cushions and eider down and swaddling.

Now the pea's presence bugged him.

Not that he could feel or in any other way personally sense its presence, but the idea rattled him that its imperfection might have in the past or might in the future bring him irritation and require him to deal with the irritation.

He decided to get rid of the little bugger. When all the attendants happened to be out of the room, the Prince ripped up all seventy-two layers of cushions and eider down and swaddling and threw them all over the floor and there it was, the little thing, hard as a little green pebble and spikey as a Lychee nut.

Because it wasn't a pea after all, but in fact a Lychee nut. The Prince decided the attendants had lied. He looked around for somewhere to put the nasty little thing.

There wasn't anywhere. There were no waste baskets in the Prince's chamber. The attendants had never allowed waste baskets for fear waste baskets would remind the Prince there was an outside world where everything wasn't so wonderful as it was for him in his Chamber.

Anyway, even outside the Chamber, the lychee nut would still exist, wouldn't it?

He put it in his mouth, but it tasted nasty and its little barbs bit his tongue, so he spat it out onto the floor.

Faced with so many insurmountable obstacles, he decided to give up.

Just then his attendants came in. The mess he had made terrified them because they knew the King and Queen would blame them and punish them for failing their Prince. They ran out of his chamber and out of the kingdom altogether, never to be seen again.

The Prince tried to put the blankets and cushions and swaddling back the way they had been, but he couldn't remember how the coverings had been arranged, nor had he ever done anything like that for himself.

After an interminable two minutes trying, he sat down and stared at his nut on the floor and wept.

All right, I confess: my grandmother never told that story to me. That's my story. I made it up. She couldn't have imagined it. She lived to be ninety-eight. In her own long life outliving several generations that came and went, not to mention a bunch of famines and depressions and wars, she never encountered a single man or boy like this Prince.

Where did you all come from?

I still hope. I will risk all to help even just one of you. I promise I am willing to meet in person to talk to any of you at any time. Call me or email me or get in touch through this Consciousness Team site. I will come in person. Please let me try to convince you.

You ask me, why do you care?

I admit it: subjectively, I don't care. But this is how God commands me to act. To help others whenever I can. So I will.

38 On The Road Again

"If you step up to the bell, you must ring it."
                    Mel Brooks, quoting Michael Hertzberg

Hack dreamed he threw a stick for Shakey to fetch but Calvin beat Shakey to it and ran back to Hack with the stick clenched in his jaws. Then Calvin grabbed the stick out of his mouth and prodded and poked Hack hard in the ribs with the end of the stick. Hack tried to fend him off, but Calvin wouldn't stop prodding and poking Hack in the same place in his ribs over and over until the place began to hurt, a little at first, but then a lot, and then Hack woke up and opened his eyes to see Mattie's smirking face above him and realized Calvin's stick was Mattie's stiff index finger prodding and poking him in the ribs. And it did hurt. A lot.

She said, "They ran away."

"Who ran away?

"Who do you think?"

"Are you sure?"

"Get your butt out of bed and come look for yourself."

He glanced at the clock. It was 7:30. "One minute, please."

She disappeared. He closed his eyes. When he opened them again it was 9:30. He got up and dressed. On the kitchen table he found a note from Mattie:

> "Working at a shift at Berringer's—back this afternoon—
> Good luck finding your pet!"
> P.S. And Shakey too!"

Hack looked out the window at the backyard hut. No Calvin. No Shakey. He boiled water and poured it into a mug and dumped in a packet of instant coffee. He dropped an ice cube into the mug to cool the coffee faster and drank the coffee, but it was still too hot, and it burned the inside of his mouth. At least the sting helped wake him.

He put on his coat and boots and went out to the backyard and saw the two sets of prints leading out of the yard to the street and into the distance.

Hack pulled his phone out of his coat pocket and called Gus.

Gus answered right away. "They're gone, right?'

"How'd you guess?"

"I know huskies."

"I suppose Calvin got restless and took Shakey with him."

"Right events, wrong emotional support animal."

"What do you mean?"

"It's huskies that get antsy and run away. They're famous for it. They like to roam free. Most likely Calvin followed Shakey, not the other way around."

"Does your canine intuition give you any insight where they went?"

"Yeah, it does. Come on out here and we'll go after them. They have to travel on foot. Since we're modern types who use combustion powered vehicles, we can maybe head them off."

Hack drove out to Gus's place. Gus was standing in his long gravel driveway, geared up and ready to go.

Hack parked and got out of his car and Gus said, "Follow me," and started hiking into the woods. Hack followed him along the path they'd used before to get to their shack. But Gus took them past the shack and headed not towards the Morty Mark mine shaft but in the direction of their winter night's campsite, out near the bear cave.

Gus was in a hurry, lifting and extending his long thick legs and plowing forward over the deepest pockets of snow. Skiing kept Hack in shape, but he had to hurry his shorter stride to keep up. Neither spoke; they saved their wind for the hard trek.

After several hours covering many miles, Gus turned a corner ahead of Hack and stopped and waited for Hack to catch up. When Hack reached Gus's side, Gus pointed.

About fifteen yards ahead was the bluff that led down to Gynodelphia.

Hack asked, "What makes you sure this is the right spot?"

"It's logical," Gus said.

"You think Calvin's going to bring Shakey here because he's hung up on Tiff?"

"I already said it. More likely Shakey's going to bring Calvin because Shakey's got Artemis on what passes for his brain."

"Dogs do that? Form romantic attachments?

"Shakey and Artemis looked pretty attached during that dog knot," Gus said. "The truth is I got no idea. Shakey's only had sex one time we know about. And if he can remember where his food comes from, he ought to be able to remember where his sex comes from too. And don't forget how powerful his sense of smell is. For all we know, Shakey knows where Artemis is every moment of every day, at least while she's in heat."

"Okay. I buy it. Shakey and Calvin are a pair of romantic dreamers drawn relentlessly to their hearts' desires and we can head them off here."

Gus and Hack took up posts on the path, waiting for the runaways. To keep warm, they paced.

When Calvin and Shakey showed up, they were hiking up the bluff from the direction of Gynodelphia.

Shakey ran to meet Gus and Hack on the path and exchanged muzzle-to-hand greetings with each. Calvin stopped about twenty feet away and stood stock still. He looked different somehow, but Hack couldn't place why. Hack read something disheartened in his facial expression and posture. Had something happened to him?

"Calvin," Hack said. "Do you know how worried I've been?"

Calvin said nothing. His eyes looked wilder than ever. His legs crumpled under him and sat into the snow where he stood. Shakey ran back to him and nestled his head against Calvin's ribs. Calvin put his arms around Shakey and hugged him. The two sang a brief low-voiced duet of whines and whimpers, then stopped.

Hack couldn't figure it.

"Calvin, I know you're in love with Tiff," Hack said. "But you can't go down there again when she doesn't want you to. That's stalking. You need to stay home with Mattie and me, where it's safe."

"Know," Calvin said. "Followed Shakey."

"Told you," Gus said to Hack.

Hack and Gus glared at Shakey. Shakey squatted down on his haunches, head cocked at an angle, pink tongue lolling, looking up at the men with eyes bright and blue.

Hack didn't buy Shakey's feeble pretense of innocence. Hack looked directly into Shakey's baby blues and told him, "You're a bad influence. When he fell in with you, Calvin fell in with a bad crowd."

Shakey bleated a short whimper.

Hack said, "I don't believe a word you whine."

In apparent response, Shakey dashed off in the direction of Mama Bear's cave.

"You hurt his feelings," Gus said.

"Good," Hack said. "He's nothing but trouble."

"And where would you be without him? He's the one tracked Calvin the last time, remember?"

Shakey came back and squatted again.

Hack pointed and asked, "What's that in his mouth? Is that some kind of sausage?"

"I'm pretty sure I don't want to know," Gus said.

Calvin stepped forward and held his open right hand in front of Shakey, who dropped the thing into it. Calvin lifted it to inspect it. He sniffed it. His eyes grew wide. He sniffed it again. He said one word: "Victor." He held it towards Gus and Hack.

Hack clutched his hands behind his back, just in case Calvin tried to hand him the thing. Out of the corner of his eye, Hack noticed Gus next to him hiding his own hands behind his own back.

Hack said, "I've only seen one of these up close, and it was my own, but I think it's a man's penis."

"I think you're right," Gus said.

"Do you think Mama Bear had something to do with this?"

Gus leaned forward until his face came within a few inches from Calvin's open hand. He shook his head. "Not unless she's taken to carrying a knife."

39 *A Limp Dick in a Baggie*

Calvin sat down on the hard ground and stared at the penis in his hand. He began to whimper again. Shakey went to the edge of the bluff and squatted and stared out at Gynodelphia. Hack and Gus argued about what to do next.

They couldn't go to the cops, not even to their buddy Rolf—a sheriff's deputy they hung out with and distrusted slightly less than the others.

After twenty minutes, Gus came up with a plan. "We'll make it a ruse."

"You mean, like a ploy?"

"You could say it that way."

"Or a stratagem or a gambit, or a dodge, maybe even a shenanigan?"

"You been staying up nights reading the dictionary again?" Gus said, "Here's what I'll do. I'll get Rolf out here in the woods on some excuse—"

"What excuse?"

"I'll come up with something."

"Like what?"

"I don't know," Gus said. "How about, my new dog is missing, and I could use Rolf's help finding him?"

"You think he'll buy that?"

"It doesn't matter whether he buys it as long as he goes along with it. And I know the man. A six pack for his trouble and he'll commit."

"Then what?"

"Then I get him out here and arrange it so Rolf finds this thing himself. We're not involved."

"Sounds lame," Hack said.

"You want to waltz into the Sheriff's office with a limp dick in a baggie?"

"Not really."

"With your soiled reputation? You think you'll ever see sunlight again? You know cops always suspect the one who finds the body."

"This isn't a body."

Gus looked around. "There's a body around here somewhere. Trust me."

40 Murder Victim Found

Ojibwa City *Savage*
Dateline: Ojibwa City
By Staff Writer Norton Shandling

Authorities have recovered the body of an apparent murder victim from the woods just outside Ojibwa City. They have identified the victim as Victor Orwell Radke. Mr. Radke was an employee of St. Paul software giant Gogol Checkov.

Possibly coincidentally, just three months ago this reporter interviewed Mr. Radke about his friend and coworker Mel Untermeyer. Mr. Untermeyer had committed suicide after becoming despondent when Gogol Checkov fired him amid sexual abuse allegations. He was unable to find new employment.

Authorities are revealing little to the public, but they do concede they are treating Mr. Radke's death as a murder and that he was mutilated. They are withholding specific details of the mutilations, in part to test for the false confessions, and in part because releasing details otherwise known only to the murderer might hamper the investigation.

The body was accidentally discovered by Ojibwa County Sheriff's Deputy Rolf Johnson, who happened upon it while in the woods helping a local citizen search for a lost dog.

The discovery of the body comes at a time when Gogol Checkov has already come under increased public scrutiny. Trial is ongoing in the case of Gogol Checkov employee Richard Kadlec, accused of an alleged terrorist murder.

Authorities have also requested help locating a homeless man recently seen roaming the woods in a strange fur costume, sometimes in the company of a white dog. Some witnesses claim to have seen him carrying a wooden spear with a stone point. Authorities have declined to name him as a suspect, but they do concede he is a person of interest in the murder, or at least a potential witness.

162

What if any role the latest victim Mr. Radke may have had in Mr. Kadlec's alleged crime is the subject of widespread speculation, some of it outlandish. None of that speculation will be repeated in these pages, the *Savage* being one of the few media outlets left in America with scrupulous editorial standards, or for that matter any standards at all. Or any scruples.

41 One Emotion Behind

"Not every problem someone has with his girlfriend is caused by
the capitalist means of production."

Herbert Marcuse

Hack read the *Savage* news article about Radke sitting in the
little easy chair in the living room, on an actual hard copy print
edition of the *Savage*. Once in a while Hack liked to soil his hands
with newsprint and ink.

He had to admit that Gus's ruse had worked to perfection.

When Hack finished the article, he crumpled up the paper and
threw it down on the floor. Another nice thing about paper—the
crumple-throwdown was something you wouldn't do with a
computer, unless maybe you were super-rich.

Mattie walked in and picked the paper off the floor and sat down
on the couch and uncrumpled it. She read it for a few minutes, then
said, "Time for me to get out of this place."

He asked, "Just because of a little murder?"

"Not just that. Dudley's sent me money for a ticket. I can head
down to Phoenix. Our tour starts in two weeks. Here, I'm doing
nothing. There, at least I can rehearse with the band. Work up some
new songs."

Hack said, "Let me show you something." He stood and walked
over to the laptop and brought the *Annals* abuse accusations and
follow-ups against Mel on the screen. He stood and motioned for
Mattie to sit in the chair. She gave him a curious look but did as he
asked.

"Read that, please," he said. While she read, Hack stood and
savored the look of her hair and shoulders. He resisted the impulse
to take a deep whiff of her scent, which he loved. What if she
thought it rude?

He did it anyway.

She ignored his poor etiquette and looked up at him. "Okay."

Hack said, "Do you believe this stuff? Is it crazy or am I?"

"Oh, it's mostly crazy," Mattie said. "But stuff does happen, and it does wear you out. Sometimes it's even dangerous. I don't know very many women who've never been poked or pawed or had something rough happen to them their whole lives."

"But is she someone with a real gripe? Or is she just capitalizing on other people's legitimate complaints for her own aggrandizement?"

"I love it when you use words like aggrandizement. It makes me feel smart just to know you."

"Please. I'm looking for a serious answer. It may connect to Sam's case."

"In case you haven't noticed, women see things different from men."

"As a matter of fact, I have noticed. In fact, I just finished a new song about it," Hack said. "I've been working on it since last summer. I think it's for a man to sing."

He fetched her old acoustic guitar from the closet and took it out of its case. He sat on his chair again and set the guitar on his thigh. She went back to her seat on the couch and waited with her hands folded in her lap while he picked and strummed and loosened and tightened the guitar pegs until it was tuned.

She never used to do that—sit patiently with her hands folded.

She said, "Funny to see you playing a guitar instead of a keyboard. I didn't even know you could."

"I can't, not really. But I only need three chords for this song, and they're the three I know. And the guitar works better for it. Think Johnny Cash or Elvis singing "That's All Right" or any of fifty other rockabilly songs."

Hack picked the bass line he had in mind.

She nodded. "Like *Folsom Prison Blues*."

"Right." Hack began strumming the standard three chords of country and blues and rock at about the *Folsom Prison* Blues tempo. He said, "I call this 'One Emotion Behind'."

He intoned,

"You tell her 'Now I get it,

I see where you're coming from'.
    She looks at you
    Like gum on her shoe
Like you're blind and deaf and dumb.
You can't help it,
You're just a man,
That's how you're designed.
No matter how you chase her
You're
One emotion behind."

Hack eyed Mattie for her reaction, but she had put her chin on her hand and was watching his guitar, intent on his song, giving him nothing back. He continued,

"She cries all through the morning
And laughs all through the night.
  She shares her feelings
  'Til your brain is reeling
Through the dawn's early light.
She can't help it.
She's just a woman,
That's how she's designed.
No matter how you sweat it
She keeps you
One emotion behind."

Still nothing coming back from Mattie. Hack launched into the bridge:

"You men out there just best beware
She'll get you on the run.
That woman will feel six feelings,
While mister
You can muster
Only one."

Was Mattie parting her lips in a reluctant almost-smile? He went back to the original tune,

"You talk right past each other
No common ground to find
　She gives you that stare
　Like there's nobody there
Like you're totally out of your mind.
We can't help it
We're only human
That's how we're designed.
No matter how we work it
You're
One emotion behind."

"I see," she said started to rise from the couch.
"Wait," he said. "There's one more verse."
"With you, there always is," she muttered, but graced him
with another a slightly warmer smile and sat down again. He
finished up,

"It happened just this morning
You knew she felt that way.
　You think you got near
　But she makes it clear
That was yesterday!
You can't help it—
You got no clue what's
Going on in her mind.
You tried so hard to keep up,
Now you're
Two emotions behind."

Hack banged out a few final chords and looked up at Mattie.
"Clever," she said. "I suppose."
"That's all?"
"It's nice," she said. "Of course, I don't see myself singing it.
You should sing it."
"You're the only singer in this house. I'm terrible."

"Just fake-sing and talk it through like you did with that that last song you wrote for Dudley, "It Ain't Gamblin' When You Know You're Gonna Lose.""

"Which went nowhere."

"Dudley likes it."

"But you don't," he said.

"Only because I thought it was a song about me, about how tough I am to get along with."

"And now you know better."

She shook her head. "I thought I did. You had me convinced for a while. But this new one is more of the same. Makes me wonder again about that other one from before."

"No," he said. "Not at all. It's not about us. It's about the general human condition. Men and women."

"Why don't you just go gay? Then you wouldn't have to deal with any woman."

Hack tried again. "The songs are just a microcosm."

"There you go, talking dirty again."

Hack persisted, "A little picture showing the big picture, you know, men and women, not understanding each other in general. It's not about you and me in particular."

"Whatever you know about men and women in general, you learned with me."

Hack couldn't help it. "Don't forget Lily."

"Smooth work, champ," she said. "Reminding me you were married before, to that kindhearted classy woman with all the money and clothes and degrees, the one who gave you your sweet beautiful daughter."

"Who dumped me," he pointed out.

"Don't stop now. You're on a roll." Her eyes were moist.

"This song is not about you and me personally," Hack said. "It's about everybody. Don't you believe me?"

Tears began leaking down her cheek.

He laid the guitar down and leapt across to her. He sat himself down on the couch to her right. He wanted to put his left arm around her, but something in her stiff posture warned him off.

She said, "I really think I better get down to Phoenix. At least I can rehearse with Dudley and the guys."

"I can't let Sam down. I've got to finish helping him with his trial. I can't go yet."

"But I can. And you'll come when you can. It'll be soon, right?"

"You're leaving because of this song?"

"No," she said. "It's a perfectly fine song. I mean that. It's got a funny angle and it's mostly true. Maybe totally true. And I believe you that it's not about just you and me. Pretty much everybody's in the same fix. Probably gay couples too."

Then she went silent. He got nothing more out of her the rest of the day, and the next day he drove her down to the Twin Cities airport and she was gone.

42 A New Turing Test

"The rifle hanging on the wall of the working-class flat or labourer's cottage is the symbol of democracy. It is our job to see that it stays there."

George Orwell

Hack was on Highway 15 driving back from the airport when his cell phone rang. It was Gus. Hack pulled over onto the shoulder. He rolled to a stop and answered.

"Your turn to help me out, Partner," Gus said. "For a change."

"How?"

"There's a wounded doe out in the woods," Gus said. "With a broken off piece of wooden spear sticking out of her. We don't need to wonder who put it there."

"Dammit."

"You're going to help me track her and finish her. We can't let a wounded animal suffer like that."

"This isn't deer season. Why don't you call the DNR or the Sheriff's office?"

"Because they won't do anything. You know that."

It was true. Every winter, food supplies dwindled. Hungry deer came out of the deep woods and crossed highways and roads, where cars and trucks hit them. Wounded deer overran the north woods. Overwhelmed authorities stopped answering the calls.

Hack started up Highway 15 again and turned off at Gus's place.

When he got there, Gus was waiting with his Winchester Model 1894 rifle.

"Grandpa's?" Hack asked.

"Great-grandpa's."

"You know where this doe is?"

"I've got an idea," Gus explained. "A snowshoer saw it and mentioned it to Mike Berringer at his café. Mike called me."

"Let's go."

Gus led Hack on the familiar path past their shack towards the mineshaft.

About two hundred yards past the shack, Hack saw the first sprinkles of blood in the snow. The sprinkles turned to bigger patches. They followed the blood trail to a small clump of trees. Hidden there they found a young doe sprawled on the ground, the broken haft of a wooden spear poking out of her haunch. She saw them and tried to drag herself away using just her front legs.

"Her back's broken," Gus said. "No way anyone can fix her up."

"And if we call the DNR?"

"They might drop by in a day or three."

"Go ahead," Hack said. He walked away about a hundred yards and covered his ears with his hands to protect his hearing. The expected blast of the rifle boomed in the woods behind him.

Gus walked out to him. "For all we know, she's been stuck out here like that for days." Gus shook his head. "Tough to see an animal suffer like that."

"You old softie."

"Shut up."

"What about the meat? You going to just leave it?"

"Nature will take care of it. I don't need the meat. There's creatures out here will make good use of it, especially in the winter. It's the natural way. Totally paleo."

They hiked back to Gus's house and went inside and took Chumpsters out of the fridge and sat down at the kitchen table.

"Tell me," Gus said, "What is going on with this idiot friend of yours?"

"You mean Calvin?"

"You got any question in your mind where that spear came from?"

"None."

"Where's the good ending for this?" Gus asked. "It's bad enough what he does to himself, but what about everybody else? Nothing and no one is safe from his stupidity, not even animals."

"At first you thought he was crazy. Now you think he's stupid?"

"What's the difference?"

"I'm not sure," Hack admitted. "After all, what is the difference between crazy and stupid?"

"Or crazy and evil," Gus said. "Three versions of the same thing."

"You might be right," Hack said. He stared at his Chumpster bottle. At the moment, he wasn't thirsty. He said, "Do you know what the Turing test was?"

Gus shook his head.

Hack said, "Alan Turing was a mathematical genius. He helped invent computers. There was an argument about whether computers could get as smart as humans, about whether artificial intelligence would ever be possible."

Gus said nothing.

"Turing invented an imaginary test," Hack said. "The idea was that you could put a screen between a computer and a genuine human being. If the real human had a conversation with the computer and couldn't tell whether it was a computer or another human, then whoever created the computer had achieved true artificial intelligence."

"How does that apply here?"

"Maybe we need a new Turing test to be able to test for any differences between crazy and stupid and evil. Three things that all look the same to me. The longer I live, the less I can tell them apart."

Gus said, "Like when a mother murders her baby or something like that, and people say she must have been crazy to do that, because no sane mother would have done that awful thing."

"Right. But maybe she's not crazy. Maybe she's evil. Or even just plain stupid and she can't imagine the consequences of her actions. In the end, how can we tell the difference? Maybe they're all just different forms of the same thing. From the other side of the screen, how can we normal human beings tell?"

"No answer to that," Gus said. "You think Calvin tortured that deer because he's crazy or because he's stupid? Or even because he's evil?"

"Maybe his craziness made him do an evil thing. Or maybe it makes him too stupid to know what he's doing."

"But before you told me he's not crazy, just logical. Now you're saying he is crazy after all."

"Maybe being too logical is a kind of crazy," Hack said.

"It's sure made him stupid," Gus said.

"Speaking of which," Hack said, "I'm feeling pretty stupid right now myself, you know, trying to figure out Mattie."

Gus snorted. "Of course."

"I finished a new song," Hack said. "And I played it for Mattie."

"I can hardly wait," Gus said. "She told me about your last one. Go grab LG's guitar and play the thing for me."

Hack hauled LG's electric and mini amp out of his room and brought them into the kitchen and hooked them up.

He banged out the Johnny Cash *Folsom Prison Blues* rhythm and chords and sang the entire song, finishing up with

> "You can't help it—
>   You got no clue what's
> Going on in her mind.
> You tried so hard to keep up
> Now you're
> Two emotions behind."

Hack hit the final three chords and looked at Gus.

Gus said, "Just to get it straight, your idea in this song is, no matter how hard you try, you can't keep up with Mattie's emotions, so you're always one emotion behind?"

"Not me and Mattie in particular," Hack said. "Men and women in general."

"And you're permanently clueless about her feelings, except at the end you're even worse off than before, because now you're actually farther behind, since you're now two emotions behind instead of only one."

"That's the song."

"And you played that song for Mattie?"

"Yeah."

"And then you told her it wasn't about her?"

"Of course."

"You expected her to believe you?"

"I hoped so."

"Just now, when you were in the middle of saying those words you wrote, did you actually listen to any of them?"

Hack said nothing.

Gus said, "Well, I'm not unusually sensitive—"

Hack cut him off. "You're not even usually sensitive."

"Didn't we already have this zinger?"

"It seemed zingy enough to reuse."

"You mean recycle?"

Now Hack moved to comfortable territory, riffing with Gus: "I'm being environmentally conscious. It's our duty to recycle the same zingers over and over. Saves the energy and resources otherwise spent creating new zingers."

As each generally did for the other, Gus caught on right away. "Maybe that's why all these GC people in those *Annals* you told me about recycle those old harebrained ideas. Don't want to foul up the world with new harebrained ideas."

"Very green of them," Hack agreed. "I mean, if I can put out a sack of used aluminum cans every week to be carried off and re-used, why not a sack of used drivel?

Gus said, "Then learned professors can come by and collect the used drivel and take it back to their universities and pour it into new containers and paste on new labels and sell it again."

"New labels, that's the ticket," Hack said. "New labels for all the old theories like socialism, fascism, communism, libertarianism, corporatism, racism, vegetarianism, and the rest of the catastrophes."

"I got it." Gus snapped his fingers. "Instead of communism, we'll call it post-modernism."

"Perfect! And instead of Nazism, we'll go with Intersectionality."

"Is that right?" Gus asked. "Intersectionality is Nazism?"

"Sure. Like Nazis, Intersectionality types divide all human beings in the world into categories based on race and religion and so on. Then they grade the categories on who's the most worthwhile and who's evil. Then, no matter how much they switch around which categories they grade high and which categories they grade low, Jews always wind up in the evil category. See? Nazis."

"I get it," Gus said. "Remind me. Why are we talking about this?"

Hack said, "I've spent the last few days torturing myself by reading all these used-up theories to help Sam, and the more I think about it, in the end it's always really just one theory, about how there used to be this golden age in the distant past and all we need for a new golden age in the future is go back to doing what we used to do back then, when there was no property and women ran things, or when everything was simpler and you grew your own carrots or killed your own deer."

"And your impacted molar sentenced you to an agonizing death," Gus said.

Hack said, "I don't think modern dentistry is part of their construct."

"But why do a few cranks matter to you so much?

"They're not just a few cranks," Hack said. "They're cranks with power. They control access to information. They're cranks who control Internet search results for millions of people. They can redirect it people down the channels they want or shut them out altogether. They can make or break powerful businesses. They can decide elections. They can cause wars."

"You really think so?"

"I really think so."

There was a pause in the conversation while the two men considered.

"Are we done?" Gus asked. "Done riffing, I mean?"

"I think so," Hack said. "I've run out of gas."

Gus said, "That'll never happen."

Hack asked, "What about the song? What do you think?"

"I think." Gus paused. He shook his head. "What do I think. You're asking me, what do I think?"

"Yeah. What?"

"About the song?"

"Yes. About the song."

"The song you just played me?"

"Yes, that song."

"If you played that song for Mattie, you may not be evil, but you are crazy. Or stupid. And you're right about what you said before. I can't tell the difference."

43 Sam At Trial: Final Arguments

The next morning, Hack sat in the back of the courtroom again and watched Prosecutor Johnson stand in front of the jury. She read from a yellow pad, "Whoever does any of the following is guilty of murder in the first degree and shall be sentenced to imprisonment for life: causes the death of a human being with premeditation and with intent to effect the death of the person."

She slammed the book shut. The noise ricocheted around the walls of the courtroom.

She said, "That's the law: causes the death of a human being with premeditation and intent. You have the Court's instructions on how to apply that law to the facts. And these are the facts:"

For the next three hours, she spelled out her case: Rick Kadlec's obsessions with weather and climate and with a movie which celebrated anarchist killing; how he planned killing Penn Lajoie over the long months; how he secretly manufactured his own saltpeter and then combined it with sulfur and charcoal to make black gunpowder; how he constructed and intentionally planted the bomb under the SUV in a way which guaranteed the death of Penn Lajoie and anyone else in the vicinity; how forensics had tied the chemical signature of the bomb that killed Lajoie to the specific signature of the home-made black powder Kadlec manufactured in his basement; his videotaped confessions and justifications.

When she finished, she said, "If this isn't first degree murder, there never was any. The Legislature was wasting its ink."

She sat down with careful dignity and folded her arms in obvious satisfaction. She had made her case.

Sitting in the back, Hack agreed with her.

Sam stood and faced the jury and said this:

A young man faces a crisis. He is a decent young man and a serious young man, but perhaps he does have one weakness: he thinks too much.

Worse, he knows too much.

He knows about the crisis rushing towards us. He knows that our opulent way of life fills the very air we breathe with carbon which threatens to inundate the world with heat and rising seas, to wreck our civilization and destroy all that humanity has built after so many long millennia of suffering and struggle. Ultimately, to return us to a dark age—if we survive at all.

This coming disaster is not some theoretical possibility. It is real. It waits just around the corner. It is imminent. Science tells us so. Our political leaders tell us so. Our religious leaders agree. All trustworthy and responsible people agree.

But the band plays on. The world sails merrily towards self-destruction, paying no attention whatsoever to this inconvenient truth.

This young man requires recognition of this truth, not for himself, but for all humanity. For all creatures on our fragile blue planet. Who among us will be able to survive the coming disaster?

But an Opponent stands in the way. An Opponent with shiny credentials and glib wit and a clever way with slippery arguments. The Opponent tempts us to ignore this terrible truth. He promises us our lives can continue just as they have been. We need pay no price for our opulence. We can continue to enjoy the plenty of our planet and pay nothing back, to be stewards of nothing but our endless avarice and gluttony, our own capacity for self-indulgence, our own greed.

Though the Opponent clothes his temptation in confusing numbers and fake facts and pseudo-scientific jargon, the naked truth is that all the opponent's arguments come down to one: do nothing.

That's right. Do nothing. It will go away. It is not there. It is imaginary. Sail right ahead: bite right into your prime steaks and your fresh Atlantic salmon and your crisp succulent strawberries they fly in every day; ride your gas guzzlers and your yachts and your private planes to self-destruction,

And the young man sees that no one is listening.

Why? Why aren't we listening? Why don't we pay attention?

Attention must be paid. If not now, when?

Like prophets of old, the young man thinks, I will make them listen. I must do something! And he does.

The prosecution says he was wrong to do what he did. They claim it was against the letter of the law. With the moral certainty of all self-styled experts on every matter, they tell us it was wrong. I do not stand here to argue with those who say that. Undoubtedly, they are wiser than me or you.

Maybe you agree with the experts. Maybe you think what he did was inappropriate. But ask yourself: if we and the law recognize the natural right of self-defense for a single individual, can there be no right of self-defense for humanity as a whole, for our planet, for our very existence?

And the young man risks all in his struggle. Our struggle. Humanity's struggle.

We all of us struggle from time to time in our lives, usually for trivial personal goals far pettier than the ends for which Rick Kadlec has fought. And who among us can guarantee that in our struggle we have always and ever used only the right tool? The appropriate tool? That we have never mistakenly taken up into our hands the wrong tool?

These are my thoughts. Whatever your thoughts may be, I ask only that you take them into account as you consider the fate of this fine young man.

44 Sarai Meets Calvin

As Hack stepped out of the court building, Hack's ex-wife Lily called and asked if Sarai could spend the night at Hack's place. She had something she needed to take care of and on short notice she couldn't find anyone else in town. Hack was happy to say yes. He picked up Sarai from school and drove her home with him. On the way, he stopped at the Ojibwa mini-Mart and picked up some groceries.

When they carried the groceries through the back door into the kitchen, Sarai called out "Mattie!" but there was no answer. She asked. "Where's Mattie?"

"Down in Phoenix," Hack said.

Sarai put her hands on her hips. "Okay, Dad. What did you do?"

"What are you talking about? Nothing."

Sarai's small dark face darkened more. "There is not an endless supply of women out there willing to marry a man like you, Dad."

"I did nothing. I told you."

"Then what's she doing in Phoenix?"

"She went down there a little ahead of me," Hack said. "To rehearse with the band ahead of that tour I told you about. I'll join her after I finish helping your grandfather with his trial."

"And that's all?"

"Yeah, that's all."

"Nothing else?"

"Nothing. I'm busy helping your grandfather with his trial and she said she wasn't doing much herself around here, so she thought she'd make it down there ahead of me and do some rehearsing. I played her my new song and she took off. And by the way, why am I explaining all this to a ten-year-old?"

Sarai always listened like a lawyer. Sam's granddaughter. "What song was that?"

"Just a song. Another song,"

"Yeah. She told me about that last song of yours—'It Ain't Gamblin' When You Know You're Gonna Lose', about this woman you met in a bar who was going to make the whole rest of your life a misery and make you pay your dues and sing the blues forever."

Did all these female people tell one another everything? Hack took a deep breath. "As I told her then, and as I am repeating to you now, that song had nothing to do with her and me. And it's none of your business anyway."

Sarai wrinkled her face in contempt, turning herself yet again into a miniature of Hack's ex-wife Lily. Hack had seen the identical expression on Lily's face dozens of times.

And in exactly the same dismissive tone Sarai's mother had used every one of those dozens of times, Sarai spoke the same dismissive phrase: "If you say so."

"I do say so," Hack said, "The song's got nothing to do with it. She already had the ticket for Phoenix when I played it for her. And it's none of your business anyway."

"Okay. So, how's it go?"

"How's what go?"

"Don't play dumb, Dad. The song."

"It's too adult for you."

"Are there dirty words?"

"No."

"Dirty deeds?"

"Of course not."

"Is it one of those country songs of yours?"

"Yes."

She regressed to her ten-year-old's smirk. "Have you considered joining the twenty-first century?"

"Not if I can help it."

"You're not going to play it for me, are you?"

"Maybe later, but first I want you to meet some fun new friends."

Hack pointed through the kitchen window to the little house in back where Calvin and Shakey lay sleeping.

"Who are they?"

"Our new guests."

"Are they the reason Mattie took off?"

"Would you get off that, please?"

Sarai said, "Isn't that just a big doghouse?"

"Sort of."

"Why is a man sleeping in a doghouse?"

"You don't remember the old song? 'Move over, little dog, 'cause the big dog's moving in'?"

"Another one of your country songs?"

"Not mine. Hank Williams."

"Never heard of him." Sarai shrugged. "You haven't told me why that man is in that house."

"Come on out and you'll meet him and you'll see." Hack grabbed a coat off the hook by the back door and jammed a pair of sneakers over his socks. He pushed the back door and the storm door open and stepped out into the yard.

Still in her outdoor gear, Sarai followed.

Hack said, "Remember, Calvin's the man, Shakey's the dog."

"That seems easy enough."

At the crunch of Hack's shoes and Sarai's boots in the backyard snow, Shakey opened his blue eyes wide. He jumped up and ran to deliver his official dog greetings. He nuzzled Hack's leg. Then he circled around Sarai, whimpering. He crouched and snuck his snout up close to her, but every time she reached out her hand, he first backed away and then slunk forward again, tail circling behind in a whirling corkscrew.

Sarai laughed, "Shakey, stand still!"

Shakey leapt forward against her chest and knocked her flat on her back and started nuzzling and licking her face. She lay giggling, trying to push him off.

Calvin had uncurled his long body out of the little shelter and stood watching. Calvin intoned, "Shakey," and Shakey backed a few feet away from Sarai and squatted and looked at her, head tilted, blue eyes shining.

Sarai got up and brushed the snow down from her hair and off her blue parka and the backs of her jeans. "Well," she commented. She looked at Calvin. "Hello, Calvin. My name is Sarai."

Calvin nodded. "Yes."

She cocked her head. "Yes, that's my name, or yes, hello?"
Calvin said "Yes," again.

Sarai looked at Hack.

Hack said, "Calvin doesn't over-talk."

"Sweet," Sarai said, and beamed her smile at Calvin.

Shakey made a feint towards Calvin and then slammed to a stop.
Calvin lunged in Shakey's direction. Shakey dodged away. Calvin
began to chase Shakey. Sarai joined Calvin and, in a moment, three
creatures were crisscrossing the yard, running in mad circles,
shrieking (Sarai), yipping (Shakey) and grunting (Calvin).

Mattie's grandfather had handbuilt Mattie's family home some
unknown number of decades ago. Later he added a concrete
platform and a raised firepit from concrete, brick and mortar. It took
up a circle about fifteen by fifteen feet.

Hack and Mattie had covered the grill for the winter. The day
was sunny, there was no wind, and the temperature had soared into
the thirties. It was a fine day to uncover the pit and cook and eat
outside.

Hack used a snow shovel and push broom to clear most of the
snow from the concrete space around the pit. He lifted the stainless-
steel cover from the grill itself and leaned the cover against the back
of the house. He laid a few pages from the *Savage* down in the grill
and some kindling on top of the paper. He retrieved bigger chunks
of firewood from the stacks in the back near the property boundary
and laid those on top of the kindling.

Calvin was still occupied with the three-man chase game and
wasn't watching. Hack lit the newsprint with his lighter and began
tending and feeding the fire. When he had some of the thicker
chunks of wood flaming high, Hack laid the metal grate across the
pit.

He got three TV trays from the house and opened them and
stood them up in open space by the pit. He set down knives and
forks and spoons on the trays. He carried three folding chairs out of
the house and unfolded them and set them in front of the trays. He
set a separate metal dish on the ground for Shakey.

He went back to the kitchen. He unwrapped the walleye filets and put the fresh whole peaches into a bowl. On a platter, he laid ten corncobs still in their husks.

He cut the peaches in half and removed their pits. He brushed the peaches with maple syrup from the pantry.

The meal was ready to cook. He brought the plates out and set them on the TV trays.

He brushed the grate with some olive oil. He laid the corncobs on the grate. After a few minutes, he laid the walleye filets next to the corn cobs. From time to time, he turned the cobs and fish with a long handled black spatula.

When Hack cooked, he used no clock. He timed by guessing— more fun that way. In a few minutes, he figured he had a few minutes left and laid the peaches down on the grate.

Before the peaches could turn mushy, he used his spatula to lift the fish and the corn and peaches one item at a time and lay them on the four plates, fair share for everyone, except Shakey got no peaches—probably bad for a dog's teeth and digestion.

He shouted "Chow!" and the three came running.

Shakey went directly for his plate on the ground and ate hands free. Calvin lifted his plate off the tray and sat cross legged on the ground and laid his plate across his lap and ate with his hands.

Sarai and Hack sat on their chairs and ate from their trays using knife and fork and spoon.

Sarai noticed Calvin's eating style. She looked a question at her father and he shrugged back. She said nothing about it. Instead, she said, "Great job, Dad. Thanks!"

Calvin grunted something that could have been a compliment or a thanks.

Shakey growled a short burst that could have meant anything ranging from "Good" to "Stay away from my food!"

After they ate, Shakey and Calvin went back to their hut and laid down and fell asleep. Hack and Sarai bused the dishes and cleaned up.

The two played chess for a couple of hours, then after Sarai insisted enough times, Hack relented and banged out and sang "One Emotion Behind" for her.

"Satisfied?" he asked.

"Dad, Dad, Dad."

"What?"

"Dad." She shook her head.

45 Calvin Hunts Again

Calvin in his house. Safe and dry and warm. Shakey fur on Calvin skin. Warm. Fur dry. Fur smell nice. Together warm.

Calvin opens his eyes. Outside, white snowflakes drift from a gray sky. Calvin shrugs off the bearskin cover and throws it away and steps out through the opening and stands straight.

Snow good. Good on skin. Hunting easy too. Animal tracks easy to see. Animals easy to find.

Shakey stands and steps out and stands next to Calvin and whines a question.

"Hunt now," Calvin says. "Hunting good," and starts walking towards the woods.

Calvin loves to walk. Calvin can walk forever, or what feels like forever to someone living in an eternal present. Shakey too.

Now is now. Calvin and Shakey are here in woods. Snows and trees all around. And snow.

How long the walking? Not a question for Shakey or Calvin. Now is now.

The snow is heavier, but Calvin doesn't mind, even when what falls on Calvin is no longer dry flakes or even heavy wet clumps, but torrents of water. Cold water. Rain. Rain that drips down Calvin's head into Calvin's eyes and onto Calvin's shoulders and down Calvin's back.

Wind hurls pellets of ice into Calvin's face and Calvin's bare legs.

Cold and wet.

Rain?

It is raining on Calvin and Calvin is wet. Very wet. Wet through, and colder. Fur pelt no help. Cold.

Calvin walks faster. Ground wet too. Trees are wet. Shakey wet too and speaking more. And more. What is Shakey saying?

Hands cold. Feet cold too, even in fur boots.

Ears hurt. Nose hurts. Neck too.

Shakey whines.

Calvin shivers. Shivers. Shivers.

Need to pee.

Calvin stops by a tree and pulls up the fur pelt to pee against the tree. Shivering.

Hands white. White the snow on the ground all around. Rain cuts holes in the snow.

Ice in the holes.

Black trees and white snow. Black fur and gray hands. Or blue?

Shakey whines always now. One big whine. Shakey noses his leg. Shakey saying something. What?

Hard to pee. Doesn't work. Want to pee but no pee.

Step away from tree, but hard to walk. Hard. Hard to stand.

Now hand blue.

Calvin inspects a hand. Why gray?

Foot gray too? Gray like blue?

Why in woods? Where is house?

Oh, Tiff.

Yes. Tiff smiling. There. Behind brown trunks. Trees. In dry green grass and black dirt and brown bark. Leaves green too. Tiff's face is a small sun. So much light. Tiff's hair dry and red. Not just red like ginger, but red like blood. And grass green. And leaves green. And black dirt after the brown trunks. So much light. So dry. And Tiff is smiling. Smiling at Calvin. Tiff. Good. She smiles. Good.

Calvin smiles back and steps towards Tiff. He gets close and she vanishes and now only cold woods and the cold rain and the cold snow on the hard ground. And the ice. Hitting him. An ice without mercy. Where is love?

His skin burns—hot! Too hot!

Skin on fire, Calvin strips off all coverings. Calvin throws the hat, the fur pelt. Calvin lifts Calvin's legs and strips Calvin's fur boots from blue feet and hurls the boots into the woods around.

Calvin is naked. Hot. Calvin raises his arms and looks up to the sky. Relief.

Then cold more. Hide?

A pile of snow covered in ice. A place warm? Dives down. Naked, burrows into the snowdrift. Water and ice and snow burn skin.

Calvin feels Shakey nestling on top. A glow of warmth on Calvin's back. Darkness.

46 Crazy Stupid Evil

In the morning, Hack drove Sarai back to school in St. Paul and came home again and parked in front of the house and went in through the front door. He spent a few more futile hours digging through the *Annals* but found nothing of interest. About lunch time, he took one look out back through his kitchen window and dialed Gus.

Gus answered, "Don't tell me. In this?"

"In this," Hack said.

"This" was the freezing rain. A blizzard is hazardous, but in the end it's just snow, even piled three or four feet high.

In Hack's bitter experience, winter rain was far more hazardous than winter snow. What starts in the upper atmosphere as moisture crystallizes into snowflakes and falls gently through a warmer layer of air where it melts back into heavy rainwater, then passes once more through the very cold air near the ground and freezes again, not back into snow, but this time into ice, coming down heavy and hard.

Ice layers all: streets and parking lots; driveways and sidewalks; rural fields and town lawns. Frozen power lines buckle and drag the electricity down with them as they droop onto the ground, crackling terrifying sparks of fire at everyone who dares come near. Trees collapse across onto roads. Branches block sidewalks.

Every surface is mortal peril. A dog can't lift its foot to take a leak without risking a hard fall and a broken leg—Hack had known this to happen.

"I'll be out there as soon as I can," Hack said.

"Don't hurry on my account," Gus said.

Hack changed into his moisture-wicking thermal socks and underwear and pulled thick wool socks and pants over them. He got into on his waterproof hooded and insulated parka and, stomping across the lawn rather than down the slippery front sidewalk, made it through the rain to his car and started it.

Hack knew how to drive in freezing rain: you set your wiper blades to the highest speed and ignore the whooshing and clattering. If your antique 1973 Audi Fox has no side defrost, you swivel your head like an owl, scouting through the wet haze for enemy vehicles that might hit you or you might hit.

Hack's 1973 antique had no modern anti-skid brakes, or even disk brakes at all—only the old-fashioned kind with pads.

So, no sudden moves. When you spot an upcoming stop sign or stop light, start pumping your brakes right away, even if it's still fifty yards off. Don't accelerate during a turn—inch your two-thousand-pound sledge around it. Point your car in any new direction before you graze your accelerator pedal, which you never jam down—you only graze it with the light caress of a concert pianist on her Steinway's sustain pedal.

Ninety minutes after the call and his starting a drive that usually took fifteen minutes, Hack pulled into Gus's yard. From a safe vantage on his back steps, Gus watched as Hack slid his Audi Fox across the yard and stopped five yards after the spot he intended.

Gus shouted, "Nice follow through!"

Hack pushed out his car door and pulled his feet up and swiveled them through the opening. He executed a vertical downward push of his boots and fastened them as well as he could onto the icy ground. Only when he felt he had sealed his boot in place did he straighten himself erect and out of the car. He closed the car door behind him. "You ready?"

"First, come inside," Gus said. He turned and went through his back door into his kitchen.

Hack knew how to walk on ice: extend one foot slightly ahead and lift it straight up and put it straight down. Then do that with the other foot. Keep doing that. You can start with your left foot and then use your right or the other way around.

Either way is okay, but that's the end of your discretion. The instant you forget and relapse into your slovenly fair-weather stride is the instant you wind up flat on your ass.

Hack made his way across the glaze over Gus's yard to Gus's back steps and up them. At the back door he took off his boots and stepped into the kitchen, where he found Gus stirring a big black skillet of hash made from steaming scrambled eggs spiced with onions and peppers and loaded with chunks of venison sausage. Already on the table were thick hunks of hot rye toast, berry jams, orange juice and coffee. Gus began ladling out the hash onto two clean white plates the size of garbage can lids.

Gus had already laid out two back packs on the floor. On a counter stood two Stanley stainless steel thermoses.

"Before we go, we fortify," Gus said. "And I figured you'd be in too much of a hurry to put your own kit together."

Hack took a chair at the table.

"We can take a few minutes," Gus said. "Could be hours if we find them."

No argument there. Gus's spread was a miracle. Hack grabbed knife and fork and chowed down.

Gus did likewise. "By the way, got any good ideas where to look?"

"Not really," Hack mumbled through a mouthful of hash.

"What's that?"

"Never mind."

Gus shrugged to show he didn't understand and didn't care if he didn't understand and turned his attention to his own plate.

An hour later the two men hoisted their backpacks and put on their boots and set off through the back door and down the back steps and across the yard into the woods.

The rain traveled along. Their eyes stung and their vision blurred. The wet dripped off their hoods and down their foreheads and froze their lashes and melted again and dribbled off their noses and down their cheeks.

From every black tree branch hung glowing ice, white mini stalactites, which clung to branches and weighted and broke them. Here and there dark columns of broken trees blocked their paths, exposing dying yellow-white wood, the only living color in this gloomy wet desert.

Through the destruction clambered Hack and Gus, over obstacles where possible and around them where necessary, slipping and sliding along whatever paths they found or could make on their own.

No tracks of man or dog could show on this glazed ground. Hack and Gus started with a checklist of places they'd found Calvin and Shakey before. They tried the shack and the mine shaft and the bluff overlooking the fields and all the paths in between. They even dared to approach Mama Bear's cave and peer in, but saw no trace of Calvin or Shakey, only a warm-looking dry bear asleep with her cubs, snug and oblivious in her home.

"Lucky old bear," Hack whispered, and Gus nodded. Mama stirred and the two men left discreetly but quickly.

Eventually they soaked through, wet and cold, because no amount of waterproofing could proof against this much moisture and no amount of insulation could insulate against this much cold.

After about three hours they took a break. They hid under the shelter of a huge fallen trunk, where they sat on the bark of a thick soaked log. They sipped their coffee from their thermoses and looked out at the rain and longed for a fire.

Hack felt the sogginess seeping through the layers of underwear and pants to the skin of his butt. "How long do you think we're going to have to do this?" Hack asked.

"I don't know."

"I hope it's not forever."

"It already is."

"Can't let the man die," Hack said.

"Or the dog," Gus said. "Just to remind you, I'm out here for my dog, not for your pal."

"He's not my pal," Hack said. "He's a witness."

"Whatever," Gus said. "I didn't come out in this misery for him. I'm here for Shakey and that's it."

"A man can't just let his dog die in the woods," Hack agreed.

"Or his witness, I suppose." Gus agreed back.

A pause as they sat and sipped coffee from their thermoses.

"I'm having the strangest week of my life," Hack said. "And that's saying a lot."

"Yeah?"

"Like Alice in Wonderland. Seeing Calvin in my basement was like seeing a white rabbit checking his pocket watch," Hack said. "I see him and I follow him down a hole into my past at GC, where I meet all these creatures saying and doing crazy things."

"You told me you were doing all your GC research for Sam," Gus said.

"Okay. Maybe I'm confusing the two things. Sam's in it too, obviously. He's the original reason I'm digging into Rick Kadlec the anarchist bomber, which leads me to my GC enemy Tiff Madden turning into Gaea Free the pretend stone age farmer, along with her bosom buddy crazy Thalassa Free, and then there's Mel the Meso suicide, not to mention the new murder victim Victor Radke, whoever killed him. Let's not forget Future Sapiens, the Psycho Utopian."

"You can't make this stuff up," Gus said.

"I'm reading all these crackpot theories and we're tracking Calvin through the woods—what is this, the fourth time? I'm losing count—and that's not even the most frustrating thing that happens."

"You mean Mattie taking off?"

"Yeah. What's going on with her? No idea."

"That's the thing that matters," Gus said. "Mattie. All the rest is just the world the way it is and people the way they are. Normal."

They sat and sipped their coffee, both staring into the rain, still dripping off the bare black branches above, onto their hoods and shoulders. Hack asked, "This is normal? Every generation spawns a bunch of crackpots?"

Gus glanced at him. "You know more history than I do. What do you think?"

"I think what I'm seeing right now in GC I could have experienced at any time, in any era. Apocalyptic visions. Nasty arguments. Destructive deeds."

Gus nodded. "Crazy visions. Stupid arguments. Evil deeds. Your big three. Crazy stupid evil."

"What is the matter with people?"

"A question for the ages," Gus said.

But there was no answering that question freezing one's wet ass off on a soaking log under the rain-dripping trunk of a dead tree. After resting a few more minutes, they stood and peered out from under their canopy and shrugged at each other and strayed out into the misery again.

The rain finally stopped. Bitter cold closed in. It was the kind of demoralizing cold that follows a winter storm, when everything wet hardens to ice and everything already frozen turns to impermeable stone.

They exhausted their list of previous Calvin sightings. For the next hours, they mapped out a comprehensive search path, relying on Gus's mental picture of the area and Hack's programming skills. They criss-crossed the woods, trying to hit every location as close as the weather and terrain would allow.

Late in the day, near darkness, Gus stopped and laid one big mitten on Hack's arm. "Hear something?"

Hack stopped too. "What?"

"Listen."

At first, Hack could separate nothing from the general sigh of the wind in the branches. Both men stood silent. After a few moments, Hack picked out a sound. It was pitched high, an extended whine, a rhythmless melody even more persistent and insistent than the sounds of wind and trees. Hack knew the voice and the tune. "Shakey?"

"I'd know that whining anywhere," Gus said. "That's my dog."

Through the brambles of broken forest, the men headed towards the sound. They broke the thinner branches across their thighs and tossed aside the thicker branches and crawled over and under the fallen trunks until, his bushy tail wrapped around his snout, they found Shakey, who at first refused to move, which made them wonder, and Gus lifted Shakey up to his massive chest and unzipped his coat wide open and brought the wet shivering creature inside and zipped it up again so that only Shakey's head poked out.

That is when Hack saw Calvin.

47 The Iceman Cometh

Calvin was a frozen slab. A truly blue man—although, as Hack inspected him, his shade was closer to a slate gray. It was something Hack had heard of but never seen.

Hack dug ice and snow from around the body to widen the hole until he could see the entire Calvin. Calvin lay on his back, his left arm curled towards his face with bent fist and his right arm extended and its fingers spread in feeble supplication. Gray teeth matching the gray of his skin showed through parted gray lips. Silver streaks of ice trailed across his dark hair and down his face to his beard and frosted his dark brows. His wide-open eyes looked up towards the hair on top of his head, as if his final conscious thought had been to wonder what he'd ever been thinking of.

Hack asked, "Why is he naked?"

Gus said, "Hypothermia victims do that sometimes. Strip off their clothes."

"Why?"

"Nobody knows. He's freezing to death and then he has a hot flash, like a woman in menopause. Maybe from blood vessels suddenly dilating after all the shivering."

"And what was he doing under all that snow and ice?"

"He dug himself down and in. They call that terminal burrowing."

"Which means?"

"Exactly what it sounds like. But nobody knows why. And the only witness was Shakey." Gus hugged the dog, whose head was poking out of the top of his coat. Shakey licked the underside of Gus's beard. Gus took it without flinching.

Hack asked, "Shakey?"

"Shakey was trying to cover the exposed parts of Calvin and keep him warm, right?"

"Didn't save Calvin in the end, though, did it?

"Shakey did his best."

"And how is Shakey himself alive?"

"Thick fur and a body designed for Siberia and the Arctic. Our wimpy little winter means nothing to Shakey."

Hack said, "I'm glad you've got your dog back, but I've lost my friend."

"Not necessarily."

Hack pointed to Calvin. "Are you kidding?"

Gus said, "Remember that woman from Lengby back in 1980?"

Hack did remember. A rural Minnesota woman whose car went off the road in twenty-below-zero weather. She walked the two miles towards a friend's house but collapsed on her friend's front porch and lay outside all night. By next morning, she had frozen solid. Her friend found her on his porch. She was too stiff for her friend and his lady for the night to fit into his truck cab to drive to the local clinic. They had to load her diagonally into the lady's sedan. The medical people couldn't break her skin with a hypodermic and they barely found a heartbeat, but over the next few days she thawed and recovered completely—no harm, not even brain damage, not even a lost finger.

Gus said, "Our own clinic's actually not that far from here."

"True." The Ojibwa County Clinic was on County 15. Hack's sense of the geography suggested it was only a few miles away.

"All we have to do is get Calvin there," Gus said.

"Without breaking off any pieces."

"I guess we'll have to be careful about that."

"Let's do it," Hack said. "What have we got to lose?"

"Just some of those pieces," Gus said.

"Then let's be super careful," Hack said.

"Okay." Gus opened his coat and Shakey jumped down to the ground and sniffed around like nothing had happened.

Hack searched through the brush for sticks to use for stretcher poles. He found two relatively straight branches more than three inches in diameter. He used his knife to cut off the ice and smaller branches and scraped at the knots until the poles were relatively smooth. He laid them parallel on the ground.

Meanwhile, Gus had lowered his pack and removed a sleeping back and unfolded it and cut four sets of holes in the bag. He laid the bag on the ground and inserted Hack's two poles through the holes.

When Gus took a step back to take a look at their improvised stretcher, Shakey walked onto it and squatted. He gazed up with his blue eyes first at Gus, then at Hack.

Hack said, "Off, Shakey."

"He wants us to test the stretcher first," Gus said. "Before we use it for Calvin. Calvin can't afford the thing breaking under him."

"You're giving that dog a lot of credit," Hack said.

"Yes, I am." Gus grabbed one end and Hack grabbed the other and they lifted together. Its middle sagged under Shakey's weight, but their stretcher held. They set it down and Shakey stepped off. He cocked his head at Hack and Gus.

"What is this, one of those dog-saves-the-human movies?" Hack asked.

"It happens," Gus said. "Dogs save people."

Hack said nothing. He knew it was true.

While Hack and Shakey watched, Gus pulled a miniature spade out of his backpack and unfolded it and began to clear a much wider area around Calvin until it was almost clear of snow and ice.

It took about fifteen minutes for Gus to clear the space. Gus said, "This should do it" and folded up his spade and put it in his pack. He hoisted on his pack. "I'll take Calvin's head."

"I'll take the legs," Hack said and bent down.

"No mittens," Gus warned. "We need a sure grip."

"You're right," Hack said. He took his mittens off and stuffed them into his coat pockets. Gus did the same.

The two men squatted down in the barren area around Calvin. Gus put his bare right hand under Calvin's head and Hack put his bare left hand under Calvin's knees. The two men interlocked their free hands under Calvin's back directly below his center of mass.

Gus gave a slow, rhythmic count, "One, two, and lift."

They lifted, and gently as they could they raised Calvin and moved him to a place above the stretcher and lowered him onto it.

When Hack slid his hands out from under Calvin, his fingers and palms stung, as if he'd lifted a giant block of ice. He realized he had. He put his mittens back on and beat his hands against his chest to warm them.

Shakey stepped forward and sniffed Calvin on the stretcher and bleated once.

"Here we go," Hack said, and each man took his end of the stretcher and lifted. Hack took the front.

"Do you know the way?" Hack asked.

"I'm pretty sure," Gus said. He looked up. "And night helps."

Hack followed Gus's gaze up through the bare black tree branches into the black sky. Night had come. The wind had cleared the sky of clouds. Visibility was perfect. Brittle cold stars were strung across the sky, beacons to steer by.

Hack found the North Star in The Little Dipper, then the constellation Draco. The constellation Orion hanging very low in the south, faraway Rigel white and bright as a nearby planet. And Hack knew exactly where he was. He knew where the Clinic was too, and there would be more rough going, but he knew the way.

48 The Clinic

Hack set a slow careful pace at the front of the stretcher and Gus brought up the rear. Twice Hack started to slip but caught himself. Shakey trailed right behind the men, for once sticking close. They crossed an old hiking trail and turned left onto it. Though the path was slippery, obstacles were relatively few, and the going on the trail was relatively easy over the two miles or so to County 15.

They stood at highway's edge. There were no streetlights on this rural highway, but the reflected white of the snow cast a mild glow everywhere. The highway itself stretched black both ways into the darkness.

"Another mile to our left," Gus said.

"I know," Hack said.

Boots crunching in the snow, they lugged Calvin on their makeshift stretcher along the left shoulder of the road, facing any traffic that might come their way. No cars came, though once a fleet of snowplows roared by and the two men hustled Calvin down the ditch off to the side and waited for the trucks to pass, then worked their way back up.

All along the highway power lines drooped on the ground like broken strands of burnt spaghetti. The men passed two abandoned pickups on their side of the road and an empty SUV on the other side.

They spoke little, Once Hack said, "Electricity's gone everywhere, I suppose."

"I suppose," Gus said. They didn't speak again until they saw the clinic a few hundred yards ahead, luminous in the darkness.

"Lights are on," Hack said.

"They've got an emergency generator," Gus said. "Probably use natural gas."

"What would the Consciousness Team say about that?" Hack said.

The neon high up on the building's brick wall read "Ojibwa County Clinic." It was set back from the highway on a little frontage road.

They trundled their burden up the black asphalt to the front car port where ambulances normally went. The automatic electric doors swung open for them and they carried Calvin into the lobby and lowered his stretcher onto the floor. Hack sat down next to Calvin and then leaned back until he lay flat on the hard floor, the back of his head only slightly cushioned by his parka hood. He heard Gus heave a sigh and lie down beside him.

Hack was footsore, backsore and legsore. His shoulders and arms ached. He took off one mitten and tossed it aside and waited for his bare hand to warm enough to wiggle his fingers. Then he used his bare hand to grasp and take off the other mitten. Shakey came over and nuzzled him and then Gus and emitted a short whimper and lay down between the men. None of the three moved for a long while.

Hack heard the click of shoes on the polished floor. He looked up and saw an upside-down face. The face belonged to a blonde woman in her forties. She asked in a friendly voice, "What's all this?"

"It's our friend Calvin," Hack said. "He's frozen."

"I meant the dog," she said. "Normally, we don't allow dogs in here. Unless he's a service dog."

"Shakey's all right," Hack said. "He's with us."

"He provides service," Gus said. "He tried to keep Calvin from freezing to death."

"I see," she said. "Is he hungry?"

"He might be," Hack said. "He doesn't say. He's frozen."

"She means Shakey," Gus said.

"Of course," Hack said. "Why didn't I think of that?"

"You're disoriented," the nurse said.

"No, he's always like this," Gus said.

The blonde woman was patient. "Well, is Shakey hungry?"

"He's always been hungry so far," Gus said.

"I'll call Doctor Robert for your friend Calvin," she said. "And then I'll feed Shakey."

A thin black medical woman and another shorter rounder red-haired medical woman came and lifted Calvin's stretcher and put him on a gurney and wheeled him into a room. Hack and Gus hoisted themselves off the floor and staggered after to watch. The medical women spoke a lot of medical terminology while they covered Calvin with two electric blankets and plugged them in turned them on to low heat. They hooked Calvin up to a bunch of other equipment. The equipment flashed and beeped a lot.

The original blonde woman came in. It turned out she was a nurse. Shakey followed her in and sat back on his haunches and observed the humans.

"Frances, there is a heartbeat now," the taller thinner medical woman said to the blonde nurse.

The nurse tried to puncture one of Calvin's gray thighs with a hypodermic needle. She held up the needle for all to see. Bent.

"Your friend is a hard one," she said to Hack and Gus. "We'll just wait a bit for this."

Doctor Robert showed up. The three women explained it all to her. Hack didn't understand much except the words he already knew, like "frozen" and "solid" and "resistant."

Doctor Robert motioned to Gus and Hack and they followed her out into the hall.

"It'll be awhile before we know," she told them. "Of course, it would be better if we were a big city hospital and had an extracorporeal membrane oxygenation machine."

"Clearly," Gus said.

Doctor Robert looked at Gus. "That's a machine that could warm and supply oxygen to his blood. But we don't have one here. So that's out."

Gus nodded sagely.

Hack asked, "So is he dead?"

"You've heard the phrase fallen cold and dead?" the doctor said. "Walt Whitman, I think."

Gus grunted. Hack took it as annoyance.

"Could be," Doctor Robert said. "But nowadays we use the phrase 'fallen warm and dead'. Until you're warm, we don't know for sure you're dead. Somehow, being frozen can shut down organs so they don't fail. It's almost a kind of hibernation."

Hack thought of lucky old Mama Bear, warm and dry in her cave.

Gus must have had the same thought. "Like a bear?"

"Not really. Even if your friend lives, there's a good chance he'll have brain damage, or need to have one or more limbs amputated."

The door opened. The tall medical women said in a low voice, "Doctor."

Doctor Robert turned and followed the tall medical woman back into the room. Hack and Gus trooped after them, arriving just in time to see Calvin's arms and legs begin at first to twitch and then burst into violent jerking movements.

"Convulsions," Doctor Robert said in a pleasant but very firm voice. "Out, please."

Hack and Gus went out to the hall again and sat down on the shiny floor and waited.

An hour later, Doctor Robert joined them outside again. "The convulsions have stopped."

"That's a good thing, right?" Hack said.

The doctor said nothing.

Hack asked, "How long does it take to know one way or the other?"

The door opened. The same tall medical woman said in the same professional voice, "Doctor."

Again, the doctor went back in, and again, Hack and Gus followed her. Calvin's eyes were open. He was staring at the ceiling.

49 Intentional but not Premeditated

"Voluntary Manslaughter?" Hack asked Sam. "What does that mean?"

Three weeks after Hack and Gus rescued Calvin, the jury finally delivered its verdict. Hack and Sam were sitting in the same seats they took every time they met in Sam's office, Sam in his swivel chair, Hack in the visitor's chair, Sam's ebony desk dividing them.

"It means it was a crime of passion," Sam said. "My client was overcome by a sudden strong impulse."

"A sudden impulse to blow someone up? Didn't it take him months of preparation and planning?"

"My client was rendered incapable of self-control for the duration of the act, including the duration of the planning."

Hack asked "Where do you get that gibberish from?"

"From the law. The law is a rich source of gibberish."

"Even about homicide?"

"The jury thought it was a homicide, sure," Sam said, "But they also understood that it was abrupt and impulsive and unpremeditated. They kept asking for instructions from the judge about lesser degrees of homicide until they got the instruction they wanted and then delivered their verdict."

"Look," Hack said. "I saw the prosecution prove how premeditated it was. And the prosecutors don't have all the evidence I gave you."

"No, they don't, and that's not going to change," Sam said. "Understand?"

"Of course. Privilege and all that," Hack said. "What's the sentence for voluntary manslaughter?

"The maximum is fifteen years."

"That's it? For killing a man?"

"Don't forget the $30,000 fine," Sam said.

"Kadlec's parents are rich, right? And thirty thousand isn't even half a year's tuition to whatever asylum turned him into the mad bomber of Minneapolis."

"Harvard."

"Should have guessed," Hack said. "Do you know how the jury arrived at this verdict?"

"It was a compromise verdict."

"They can do that?"

"It was eleven to one for conviction on first degree murder. One juror was determined to acquit altogether and wouldn't budge. After many days the jurors decided they didn't want to wind up having wasted the whole trial and all those days of deliberation. So they compromised."

Hack remembered the jurors. He supposed he shouldn't judge by stereotypes, but it was hard to resist guessing which was the holdout juror—probably young Mr. Manbun—the effete indifferent one with the tattoos.

"Do you count this as a win or as a loss?" Hack asked.

Sam said, "A win, of course. No life imprisonment."

"Are you pleased?"

"I like to win," Sam said.

"So do the rest of us," Hack said. "We like it when courts lock up murderers forever. We consider that a win."

Sam said, "You'd actually feel safer if they locked up this one young man for the rest of his life?"

"Absolutely."

"You think he'll be rehabilitated in prison?"

"I don't care," Hack said. "I don't care whether he's rehabilitated. I don't care about him at all. I just want him put somewhere he can't blow up more people."

"To you, that's justice?"

"Absolutely."

"Me too," Sam admitted. "Actually."

"But you also want to win."

"I said that." Sam admitted. "And since we're asking each other questions, I have one for you."

"Go ahead."

"Have you figured out why GC expunged all its data on Calvin and Tiff Madden and you and the others? Was it fear of criminal or civil liability? Or fear of bad PR?"

"No, I don't think it was fear at all. I think it goes back to this Future Sapiens person, with all those big plans for America."

"I read his stuff," Sam said. "Fascism."

"Really? That's a pretty strong word,"

"Sure. Of course, he can't call it that. All that twentieth century unpleasantness gives the word a stink. He can dress it up as progressivism or whatever. But he wants to run America the way Xi runs China. Even justifies it with the same arguments."

"Well, regardless whether you label his Social Credit System progressivism or fascism or some other ism, Mr. Future Sapiens wants GC to build it and control it," Hack said. "That would catapult GC past Google and Facebook and all its other big tech competitors."

"Right. And the entire Consciousness Team is an obvious liability to GC and that plan," Sam said. "As Rick Kadlec just showed."

"Right. Best to pretend Calvin and Gaea and the others never had anything to do with GC."

"Any idea who Future Sapiens is?" Sam asked.

"Maybe. A guy named Frederick Sauer founded GC. Same initials—FS—so maybe it's him. He was always a kind of visionary."

"But you don't know that."

"It doesn't matter," Hack said. "I think we both know how to stick it to him and to the whole GC company."

"You mean, sneak the feds those personnel files you hacked?"

"Do you know anyone there? I mean, more trustworthy than MacNutt and Blanding?"

"No need," Sam said. "All those FBI guys are glory hunters. Those two will do just fine."

50 This is ZNN: The Holdout Juror

On camera is a middle-aged woman wearing a gray skirt and jacket and white blouse. She blinks at the camera through rimless glasses. Her gray hair rounds to a pudding bowl shape. Long bangs cover her forehead.

(Voice over from Lauren Goodwell): We're with Frances Drebin, one of the jurors in the recently completed trial of Rick Kadlec. Good afternoon, Ms. Drebin.

Frances: Good afternoon, Lauren.

Lauren: You are the so-called "holdout" juror whose refusal to buckle under to revenge-minded jurors eventually led to the compromise verdict?

Frances: That's true.

Lauren: Can you explain your reasoning for our viewers, please?

Frances: Rick is a decent young man, I mean a very fine young man. What was he supposed to do? There is a crisis, and it must be dealt with. And no one in authority seems to deal with it, so he had to do it himself. We can't allow things to just go on and on as they have, with climate change and all.

Lauren: Well, you're certainly right that we can't let climate change just go on and on.

Frances: Rick is a misunderstood young man. He made a cry for help, but no one in authority wants to help. They just want to lock him away forever. We have to send a message to those in authority. We can't just let them lock all our young people away. To do what? Rot? That's just wrong. What chance will he have then? What kind of future? We have to send a message.

Lauren: Those who disagree with you may ask, what kind of future does Penn Lajoie have?

Frances: That awful man. With his glib sneaky way of talking. He punched Rick in the face. Can you imagine the humiliation? To be punched like that in the face?

Lauren: I see what you mean.

Frances: Rick has suffered enough already. He's already in jail. He's lost his job. He's publicly shamed. It was a cry for help. What he needs is some help. We must send a message. Don't lock our young people away forever. With this sentence, he can get some help and eventually resume his place in society.

Lauren: We can all hope for that. Thank you, Frances.

Frances: Thank you, Lauren.

51 Yukky Homo

Lying on his back in a hospital bed, Calvin's mind is now clear. He remembers.

It was that night Shakey led him away from their hut to the farm where the Neos lived. Calvin had followed Shakey because he wanted to see Tiff. He loved her. He didn't remember why.

But it was Shakey. Shakey had been leading him.

It was a cold night and bitter and the only light came from the snow drifts. Bare black branches on the trees. They went down the bluff onto the path to where the women lived.

They passed the little "Gynodelphia" sign and reached the houses. The windows were all dark.

The dog Artemis came and sniffed Shakey's rear and Shakey sniffed back and the two dogs went away together.

He heard voices. A man and a woman. He walked towards the sound. It came from a small shed. He snuck up to the shed and peeked in. The man was Victor from GC. The woman was Carol. Only now she was Thalassa. They were sitting on two small crates, drinking tea. They were arguing. Calvin leaned his head against the outside shed wall and listened:

Carol: Why you come here?

Victor: I told you. I came here to talk sense into you. I told you. It's my obligation. To give you a chance. To come to your senses.

Carol: We know you the VOR dude in the *Annals*.

Victor: So? I never hid that.

Carol: Then why use the name "VOR?" You got real name.

Victor: Those three letters "VOR" stand for my name Victor Orwell Radke, and also for my handle in the *Annals,* Voice Of Reason. You people need a voice of reason. And you're one to talk. You call yourself "Thalassa," but we both know your real name is Carol Smith.

Carol: Now you deadnaming me.

Victor: That name isn't dead. What does it say on your driver's license? On the checks Gynodelphia cashes from somewhere?

Carol: Going to misgender me next? Use the wrong pronoun?

Victor: F*ck thee.

Carol: Who paying you? Exxon? Aramco? I know it someone from Big Oil. Or maybe a coal company.

Victor: No one's paying me. Who's paying you?

Carol: Me? What are you talking?

Victor: You want to shut down American energy, right? Maybe you're doing Putin's bidding. On behalf of Russia. American drilling lowers the world price and hurts Russian profits. Putin subsidizes Hollywood so-called environmentalists all the time. Pimps them. Or maybe the Arabs. So who pays you?

Carol: That's offensive.

Victor: So what? My point is what I just said makes about as much sense as what you said.

Carol: Better be careful.

Victor: The truth is no one in the real world cares enough about our puny little GC Consciousness Team to give us a dime. The Russians don't know we exist. Exxon doesn't know we exist. If they did, they wouldn't care.

Carol: All you say dangerous.

Victor: I can't say what I think?

Carol: Not if it make others feel unsafe.

Victor: Why should how you feel control what people say? You think the whole world revolves around the way you feel? That how you feel is a matter of life and death?

Carol: Is for you.

Victor: No it isn't. You and your Neo crap. The world isn't going to follow you. The world doesn't want to go backward in time, back to farming with wood and stone tools. To destitution. To back breaking labor. Not even a plow or a wheel. No medicine. No

dentists. No double cheeseburgers. You can't defeat modern
technology with stone tools and bad farming.

Carol: How about tea?

Victor: Tea?

Carol: You ought be more careful where you drink your tea.

Victor: What do you mean?

Carol: See? Neo poisons still work! Western water hemlock.
From our own garden. Farmed it myself. Grew it last summer! And
you say I can't farm! But can and did. Hemlock goes way back.
True foremother poison. A true Neo poison.

Victor: What are you trying to do, kill me?

Carol: I already have.

Victor: What for?

Carol: Revenge!

Victor: Revenge for what?

*Victor rushes out of the shed. Carol follows. He rushes at her,
but Carol dances away.*

*Calvin couldn't move. His legs froze, his arms froze, he stopped
breathing.*

Carol: I got you! I got you! You can't win! Raper!

Victor: I never raped anybody.

Carol: Rape apologist! And spy too! Squealer! Snitch! Traitor to
Mother Earth! I got you!

(Victor staggers around.)

Carol *(singing and dancing)*:

> Payoff's gonna hurt
> When this rapist bites the dirt!
> Payoff's gonna hurt
> When this rapist bites the dirt!
> Payoff's gonna hurt
> When this rapist bites the dirt!

Victor falls down. Carol stops singing and picks her knife out of the belt under her robe. She bends over him.

Calvin sees all that follows but stays frozen, unable to move until she is done and gone.

52 Visiting Calvin

Calvin had moved to St. Paul's Rush hospital. Hack and Gus drove down in Gus's truck and visited him there.

After checking in at the front desk, they rode the elevator to the third floor and walked down the corridor towards Calvin's private room.

As they approached, a thin older woman came out óf the room and closed the door behind her. She wore dark blue slacks and a cream cashmere sweater. She looked at them. "You're Hack Wilder and Gus Dropo, right?"

"Yes," Hack said.

"I'm Dolores Bagwell, Calvin's mother. You saved his life, didn't you? I can't thank you enough."

"We did what friends do," Hack said. "How is Calvin?"

"Much better," she said. "Of course, he'll need more treatment."

"How long do you think he'll be here?"

"Oh, not here," she said. "Back home in San Francisco. I'll fly him out this afternoon."

Gus asked, "So he's ready for travel?"

"We'll use the family jet," she said. "It will be much more comfortable. And we can have our Dr. Adams—he's our family physician—on the flight with us, of course."

"Of course," Gus said.

"And once he's home, Dr. Adams can administer more therapy and treatments there under the proper supervision and conditions."

Hack asked. "I thought he'd recovered. He still needs therapy?"

"Not so much from this latest incident. His electroconvulsive therapy. From before. I suppose Calvin told you about that?"

"He never mentioned it," Hack said.

"Yes, back home. It was necessary. It helped a lot, at least at first. But Dr. Adams says occasional re-administrations are necessary. It's all part of a continuing course of treatment."

"I see," Hack said.

Gus asked, "When did these treatments start?"

"Long ago," she said. "Before he moved out here. He had other issues. And we tried all kind of treatments and therapy."

"I see." Gus looked at Hack.

She smiled again. "I've got to go make so many arrangements. We'll be so glad to have him back with us. But so many thanks. I just know Calvin will be thrilled to see you both." She touched her fingertips to each man's arm in turn and hurried away, heels clacking on the hard rubber floor.

They watched her go. "Electroconvulsive therapy," Gus said to Hack. "Is that the same as electroshock?"

"I think so."

"You can get away with anything if you just put the word 'therapy' after it," Gus said. "Why not waterboarding therapy?"

"I think they had that," Hack said. "They called it hydrotherapy."

"And thumb-screw therapy?"

But Hack didn't feel like riffing with Gus just that moment. He sighed and turned and opened the door. They went into Calvin's room.

Calvin looked up from his bed. He was reading a big book with a colorful cover. As he laid it down by on the bed, Hack caught a glimpse of the word "Biomagnetism" in the title.

Calvin looked at Hack. "Hack," he said.

"Hi, Calvin," Hack said. "How are you?"

"I really don't know yet," Calvin said. He glanced at Gus. "Hello, Gus."

"Hello."

"I heard you guys saved my life," Calvin said.

Hack shrugged. Gus did likewise.

"Well, thanks," Calvin said.

"You're welcome," Hack said. Gus nodded.

Hack had to ask. "I'm curious. Can you answer a question for me?"

"Go ahead," Calvin said.

"Hack asked, "Did you learn anything from your experience? Of doing paleo and all that?"

Calvin smiled a cagey smile. "I did learn something very significant."

"What's that?"

"I know what it's like to be dead."

Almost automatically, Hack recited the next line: "I know what it is to be sad."

Calvin said, "What?"

"An old Beatles song," Hack explained.

"Really," Calvin said. "But do you? I mean, do you know what it is to be sad?"

Gus put in, "We all do."

"I suppose," Calvin said. "You know, I'm really glad you dropped by, and I don't want to be rude, but I'm really tired. I just had to deal with Dolores, and she'll be back, and she always tires me out. I love her to death, but she can be exhausting."

"Dolores?" Gus asked.

"His mother," Hack said. "You just met her two minutes ago."

"Got it," Gus said.

"Well, thanks again," Calvin said. He looked at Hack and Gus, his bright blue eyes expectant. "I really mean that."

Then Calvin said, "There's something else I need to tell someone about. I've been remembering it over and over."

"Okay," Hack said.

"I've been remembering it all in this bed. Going over it in my mind. When I was out there I saw something one night. Out in the woods. I couldn't tell anyone at the time. I didn't have the words. I don't know if anyone would have believed me anyway. And I don't know whether it was real or it was some kind of dream or hallucination."

"What did you see?" Gus asked.

"I think I saw Carol Smith kill Victor Radke."

"Carol Smith?" Gus asked.

"Thalassa Free," Hack said. "She was waving that knife at you in Gynodelphia."

Then Hack asked Calvin: "You sure?"

"No," Calvin said. "But I think so. I think she poisoned him."

Hack asked, "Why tell us? Shouldn't you tell the police?"

"I'm not sure they'll believe me," Calvin said. "The way I was, I mean. I'm not sure it's true."

"Well, it is true Victor Radke was murdered," Gus pointed out. He and Hack exchanged glances.

Hack recalled Calvin's and Shakey's whimpering episode that night after Gus and Hack found them coming back up the bluff from Gynodelphia. Had they been reacting to a murder they'd witnessed?

"We'll figure out something," Hack said. "We just came here to make sure you're okay."

"I am okay," Calvin said.

A pause.

"Well," Calvin said.

"Well," Hack said. Gus said nothing. Calvin cast a not-very-secret sidelong glance at his book on the bed beside him.

Hack and Gus took the hint and left.

As they drove back to Ojibwa City, Gus asked, "Just how are you planning to get the cops into it this time?"

"Looks like we're going to need another ploy."

"You mean a ruse?" Gus asked. "Rolf again?"

Hack said. "Maybe this time we can just give him an anonymous tip."

"He keeps cracking cases, he'll be Sheriff in no time."

"Might work out pretty well for you," Hack said, "Being personal friends with the Sheriff. Especially with your sketchy ways."

"That's a thought," Gus said.

"I'm sure you already thought it," Hack said.

After another few miles, Gus said, "I liked Calvin better before."

"You didn't like him at all."

"True."

53 Local Deputy Cracks Murder Case

Ojibwa City *Savage*
Dateline: Ojibwa City
By Staff Writer Norton Shandling

Ojibwa County authorities have claimed a breakthrough in the case of the mysterious murder and mutilation of Victor Orwell Radke, an employee of St. Paul software giant Gogol Checkov.

Yesterday they arrested a local woman named Carol Smith, a former Gogol Checkov employee and participant in what was a local all-woman community calling itself "Gynodelphia," where Smith went under the name "Thalassa Free."

Gynodelphia abruptly closed down last week after the landowner Tiffany Madden legally changed her name to Gaea Free, sold the underlying real estate, and left to write superhero movie scripts for a major Hollywood studio.

Authorities charge that Ms. Smith poisoned Mr. Radke and then dismembered Mr. Radke with a flint knife. Authorities have not publicly identified a motive. So far, authorities have not charged anyone else in the crime.

According to authorities, credit for the arrest goes to Ojibwa County Sheriff's Deputy Rolf Johnson, who himself received an anonymous tip. Coincidentally, it was the same Deputy Johnson who originally discovered the victim Radke's body while searching the woods for a lost dog.

Acting on the tip Johnson received, the Sheriff's office raided Ms. Smith's former house in Gynodelphia. They say they found significant forensic evidence, including a supply of hemlock, the poison found in Radke's various remains and in trace amounts on saucers and cups, including one cup also containing traces of the victim's DNA.

Authorities also claim to possess additional evidence but have not yet released a description to the media. Confidential sources report that some of the unreleased evidence has to do with the victim's DNA being found on a flint knife also found in Ms. Smith's possession.

Ms. Smith denies guilt, claiming she needs the hemlock as a pharmaceutical aid in the practice of her religion. After Gaea Free's abrupt exit from the scene, Smith assumed the role of as Gynodelphia's sole ShaWoman. Smith adds that her flint knife merely expresses her desire for all people everywhere to return to the more authentic lifestyles of ancient times.

Smith's attorney Sam Lapidos refused comment.

Perhaps coincidentally and almost simultaneously, federal authorities also held a news conference yesterday, announcing they are charging the Gogol Checkov company and its CEO Frederick Sauer with a myriad of tax and other violations stemming from the software giant's allegedly fraudulent employee record keeping.

With Agent Andrew MacNutt standing by, FBI Agent James Blanding spoke to a crowd of journalists on the steps of the Federal Building in St. Paul. "We are very proud of our crack team of cyber-specialists. After a long and thorough investigation, the team has identified a host of federal violations by Gogol Checkov." He then detailed a list of alleged GC criminal behavior.

Gogol Checkov founder and CEO Frederick Sauer issued a one-sentence statement: "We deny any wrongdoing."

Although the murder arrest and the federal indictments happened on the same day, it is not clear yet what if any connection exists between them, or what connection these new cases might have with the recently completed trial and voluntary manslaughter conviction of Gogol Checkov employee Richard Kadlec.

54 Have You Been Paying Any Attention At All?

Gus said, "This house is really empty without Mattie in it," Gus said.

"No kidding," Hack said.

"And cold, too. Gus said. "And empty."

"You mentioned that."

Gus nodded. "An empty bed. And cold."

"I get it," Hack said.

The two men were sitting next to each other on the couch in Mattie's tiny living room, sipping their Chumpsters while they watched ZNN in case the network showed them. They had stood in the back of the crowd watching Blanding and MacNutt's News Conference to make sure the FBI got things right. Gus was hoping the news cameras had picked them up.

Hack didn't really care—he'd had his lifetime's fill of ZNN—but Gus insisted they watch just in case. Gus had never seen himself on TV.

Hack complained, "It'll be hours before they run any clip with us in it."

"No," Gus said, "ZNN recycles the same few loops over and over. Cheap bastards."

Gus was right. Hack had to suffer through only about fifteen minutes of ZNN's alternate reality before ZNN ran Blanding and MacNutt's news conference.

At one point, as Blanding babbled on, the camera panned back to show the entire crowd.

"There we are," Gus said. "Cool." He hit the remote's pause button and froze the picture.

Hack spotted his own face in the crowd, and standing next to him, Gus.

"Hey!" Gus leaned towards the TV. "Am I really that big?"

It was true. Gus dwarfed the dozens of other people in the group shot, not only vertically but horizontally.

"Damn," Gus said.

Hack commiserated. "They say the camera adds twenty pounds."

Gus shook his head. "Must have been a three-camera shoot."

"Looks like you just zinged yourself," Hack said.

Gus sighed. He set his empty Chumpster bottle on the little coffee table and stood. "Just beating you to the obvious zinger. Well, I'll leave you to your cold empty house and even colder and emptier bed."

"You got something better?"

"I got Shakey."

Gus left and Hack flicked off the TV and got up and dragged himself from the little cold living room to the little cold bedroom.

He didn't bother to glance out the window into the snowlit dimness. He knew it was still January. The bare black branches were still out there.

Hack fell face down onto the coldest and emptiest bed he had known in a year and closed his eyes and fell asleep in an instant.

He woke up lying on his back, a woman's soft hand on his chest, her warm naked breast on his shoulder, her sweet breath on his cheek.

"Are you blowing on my cheek?" he asked.

"Yes," she said.

"Am I awake?'

"You tell me," she said.

"What's your name again?"

She nipped his ear just enough to sting. "You'd better know."

Her hand and her body and her presence warmed him. He wriggled and nestled himself up against her as close as he could get.

"Don't knock me out of bed," she said.

He said, "I thought you were in Arizona getting ready for the tour."

She said, "The tour doesn't actually start until next week, remember?"

"Did something happen?"

"Like what?"

"Like something with Dudley?

"What do you mean?"

He sighed. "Dudley's a pretty mellow guy. If you've had trouble with him, maybe…"

"Maybe what?"

"Did you say or do something?"

"That's what you think of me?"

"Lately you haven't been yourself, is all."

She said, "As a matter of fact, it's got nothing to do with Dudley. I realized I wanted to be here with you after all. Why waste a moment we can be together?"

"That's sweet," he said. "Any particular reason just this moment?"

"Have you been paying any attention at all?"

"Always."

"And you don't know? You haven't figured it out?"

"Maybe," he said. "It's very hard for us to be apart, even for a day. At least for me."

"Me, too."

"I know. Life without you is like a northern January sky, an endless grayness, a mundanity and an inanity both. One pointless day after another. Nothing changes and nothing happens, at least nothing good. It's all winter all the time, and the best I can hope for is to hunker down waiting for the next blizzard to blot out the endless gray sky."

"Wow," she murmured. "Aren't you the one. Poetic, almost."

"Just honest."

Neither said anything for a few moments. Hack closed his eyes. He was drifting back towards sleep when Mattie said, "There's something else."

"What's that?" He kept his eyes closed.

"You got no clue, do you?"

"Probably not."

"Can you read anything not flashing in green letters on a black screen?"

He didn't bother to reopen his eyes. "Occasionally. Anyway, nowadays we use black letters on white screens."

"Mister Master Detective? Mister Unlicensed Investigator? Mister blind and deaf and dumb?'

"What?

"Isn't that what I'm supposed to call you, according to that stupid song of yours? Blind and deaf and dumb?"

"Sort of. But in my song—the song which, when I played it for you, you called 'clever' and not 'stupid'—and by the way, the song tells a generic story not about you and me personally—in my song, you only think those words, you don't actually say them out loud."

"You know I can't think anything without saying it."

"True."

"You don't recognize the most obvious clues in the world, do you?"

"What are you talking about?"

"I'm pregnant."

Hack bolted upright. He inspected at her face in the dim light. She was inspecting him back, the way she did, like he presented some kind of mystery, which he knew was ridiculous, since no one could be any more obvious and transparent than he was. He was the most obvious and transparent man in the world.

She asked, "Are you happy?"

"Are you kidding? I'm elated. I'm ecstatic. I'm deranged."

"Why?"

"Are you serious? You're asking why be happy about having a baby?"

Her expression changed from puzzled to somber. She said, "That's always the question, isn't it?"

In his entire life, he'd never been asked this question. Why have a baby? The best answer he could come up with on the spot disappointed even himself. "They say the world must be peopled."

"That's it? A theory?"

"Life is not a theory." He lifted himself and crossed over to position in pushup position above her, not quite touching. So she could get a good look at his face and his seriousness.

He kissed her once on each cheek, for the thousandth time marveling at all this softness on such a tough woman. He lifted his right hand off the bed and held himself aloft with just his left hand and arm. He laid his right palm on her warm naked belly.

It was the same belly, but it felt different as it could possibly be.

As if he had never felt her belly before.

He replaced his right hand on the bed beside her and lowered himself down and kissed her where he thought the baby must be. He lifted himself back up with the familiar delicious salt taste, light on his tongue.

As if he had never kissed her belly before.

He turned his head and laid his right ear down where he thought the baby must be.

She lay through it all unmoving. "It's too soon to feel anything inside me," she said. "Or hear anything."

"I hear something," he said. "And I feel it too."

He rolled from above her onto his back again, next to her. She turned towards him and laid her arm across his chest again and leaned her cheek against his shoulder.

He spoke upwards towards the ceiling, "I don't need any theory. Babies are the best. The very best. They just are."

"You know this?"

"Yes. And so do you."

"How?" She asked. "How do I know this?"

"Because you're normal," he said. "We're normal human beings. Normal living creatures. This is one of those things we all know, maybe the most important thing all us normal living creatures know. The way we know how to breathe, how to eat, how to love. We need babies even more than they need us."

"I know that's true," she said.

"You know."

"And I also remember. I do remember." Her whisper was hoarse. "That's why I went to Arizona. To remember on my own. Somewhere else far from this place."

"Was it hard to remember through so much pain?"

"Yes," she whispered again. "It was very hard."

"You're a tough woman."

She sighed. "If you say so."

He asked, "And now you're not afraid?"

"Of course I'm afraid," she said. "So what?"

"The world is scary and dangerous. Terrible things happen." He said that and regretted it instantly. Like she didn't know that. Stupid.

In the silence which followed Hack was thinking of the terrible things people like Rick Kadlec and Carol Smith did. And of the terrible things that just happened for no apparent reason and the people they happened to, like Mel Untermeyer and Victor Radke. And Mattie.

And her lost Teddi, whom he had never even seen. With a sudden ache he wished he had. What was Teddi like?

She said, "I only wish I had your confidence."

"You have me. The confidence comes no extra charge."

"Thank you."

"You're welcome."

There was a silence between them, but it was a comfortable one.

She spoke now in her full voice, out loud, as one makes a bold declaration. "You know," she started to say something but stopped.

Hack waited for her to finish. There was no hurry.

"You know," she said after another while, "This house is too small for us and a baby too."

He said, "A practical question."

"Those count," she said. Simple as that, as if one woman and one man had now worked out together the answer to every question and every doubt any human being ever had or ever could have, about babies or the risks that come with living or for that matter, about any catastrophe that might launch itself at them out of the black void that was their future.

The next instant she was breathing soft regular breaths and Hack knew she had gone to sleep besides him, her head against his arm, her own arm thrown across chest, her hair feathering his shoulder, the fragrance of her filling the air of the tiny room.

Hack did not sleep. He lay unmoving on his back and stared up into darkness. Sometime in the night came one terrifying moment when the drumming of his pulse rose and thundered in his ears. He tried closing his eyes, but either way, eyes open or closed, he continued to see only the black void and to hear only the crescendo of the surging beat, as his heart threatened to burst through his chest.

He closed his eyes and laid his hand over his heart and concentrated on slowing his breathing. After a time, the pounding subsided back to the normal resting pulse of a normal resting man.

After another long while the morning sunlight streamed through the window into his eyes. As smooth and quiet as he could make himself, he slid from under Mattie's arm and from under the covers and set his feet on the floor.

He had fallen into bed still wearing his jeans and tee shirt. He picked a flannel shirt up off the floor and began to put it on.

Mattie lay still facing the empty spot where he had lain beside her, breathing her soft breathing and smiling her mysterious smile.

She half opened her eyes. She murmured, "Where you going?"

"To clean up my house," he said. "We're going to need the space."

She closed her eyes and he was on his way.

THE END